I0817878

TIMELESS TERROR

Second Edition: December 2023

10 9 8 7 6 5 4 3 2

Vecteezy.com

Novels By Bernard Cenney:

SPARROW'S TEARS

CLOSE YOUR EYES AND SEE

TIMELESS TERROR

TIMELESS SOLDIER

TIMELESS EMBRACE

TIMELESS DESTINY

TIMELESS TERROR
BERNARD CENNEY

AUTHOR'S NOTE:

This literary manuscript is entirely a work of fiction. Any similarity or resemblance to businesses, organizations, places, names, characters, real persons, incidents, or events is purely coincidental, unintentional, imaginary, or used in a fictitious manner.

IN MEMORIAM:

JAMES B. CENNEY
19 OCT 1989 — 11 OCT 2004

LOVED FOREVER

Send your tax deductible contributions to find a cure for children's hypertrophic cardiomyopathy to:

www.childrenscardiomyopathy.org

Thank you.
Bernard Cenney

DEDICATION:

Special thanks go to my wife, Kongsri Cenney.

Over thirty-seven years ago in Southeast Asia, Kongsri left her family, her country, and everything that was familiar to her in order to marry a young American Special Forces Captain. She took my hand and never looked back. We have supported each other in conflict and peace, hardship and success, sorrow and joy. Through it all she has loved me unconditionally and never left my side.

Bernard Cenney
Lt. Colonel (Retired)
United States Army
8 January 2024

CONTENTS

PREFACE

Perhaps someone who is mourning will find solace in the following.

The worst experience to suffer is the death of your child.

The hypertrophic cardiomyopathy death of my fourteen-year-old son, James Cenney, was a tragedy that nothing in this present world can ever make right. James was young, innocent, and just starting life. One day he was playing his guitar; the next day he was not. One day he was playing football and exercising; the next day he was not. One day he was going to school, laughing, and joking; the next day he was not. One day he was here — the next day he was gone. No father should outlive his child.

James' unexpected death shattered my wife, my daughters, and me. Parents who lose their child never bounce back. Speaking for myself, his death eroded my spirit, my resiliency, my resolve, my fortitude, my joy, my hope, and my self-worth. It became impossible to feel any sort of happiness for years.

The sheer madness and incomprehensible horror of his death destroyed my understanding of a loving God. Suffering became a daily companion. I convulsed at the clichés of "all things happen for a reason," or "God never gives us any burden we can't handle." I avoided those who declared they were "blessed by God." It made me feel as if my life was surely cursed by him.

I had seen death before, privately and in my military career. But this was intensely more personal, more visceral, more agonizing. Surely God did not want this to happen; surely God was mourning just as we were; surely God was in despair over this tragedy; surely God — as my father — empathized.

I started to have vivid dreams and visions of James. I documented and kept a record of them all. I could never (and still can't) control the mental image of my son James passing away. I have always (and still do) blame myself for not being able to somehow save him. It became an unimaginable situation. It began replaying itself, over and over, every day of my life. I was in a very dark place.

The military community at Fort Sam Houston provided us with overwhelming support. Group and individual therapy was helpful at first, but soon was not enough for me. Depression developed into apathy to even want to wake up. A terrible schism evolved between wishing for nonexistence, and a father's obligations to the rest of his family.

I just couldn't believe that James had passed away. Sometimes I think he will walk through the door, and everything will be as it once was. After he died, I thought the world would end. In my mind, I waited for the end to come. But it didn't. People went to work, children went to school, and life kept grinding on. My mind tore to pieces over whether to stop moving or to keep pushing onward.

My wife and daughters were suffering terribly as well, perhaps even more than me. Together as a family, we comforted and supported each other. I don't believe it would have been possible for me to move on without the love of my family. I felt that I had to show strength for them. I had to be the father to push everyone onward and hold the family together. If I gave up, I would have failed everyone. I knew that I had to control my grief and move forever onward. These were the thoughts constantly pounding through my mind.

James' death started me to think deeply, perhaps for the first time in my life, and to read incessantly. I read *The Upanishads*, *The Tibetan Book of the Dead*, and *The Bible*. I studied the Greek historians and philosophers: Aeschylus, Aristotle, Epictetus, Herodotus, Plato, and Sophocles. I read works by Billy Graham, Dalai Lama, Deepak Chopra, Dr. Melvin Morse, and Dr. Raymond Moody, to name just a few. I devoured just about any book that dealt with the subject of reincarnation and life after death. *The New Testament* was the enlightened example to me that life is suffering, and you must force yourself through the pain and move forward.

Pain and suffering must be understood and fully absorbed. You cannot deaden the feelings. You cannot even attempt to understand life without suffering. The message I gleaned from *The Gospel of John* brought hope to me. Sometimes a spiritual transcendence can occur from experiencing intense sorrow.

What I understood for myself was disconcerting. Tragedy strikes everyone. Those who think they are immune, only have but to wait. It will come. More tragedy is lingering around the corner. Life is the great equalizer. You cannot barter for a better life. You must push on through tragedy with all the strength you have inside. Despite unanswered prayers, you must forever move forward and do what's right. To be alive is to have constant pain and struggle.

You must push yourself forward. You must pray. You must master discipline. You must keep focus. You must practice compassion. You must hone understanding. You must think. Learn to speak less, and listen more. Put others first and yourself second. Try to help as many people as you can in your life, and if you can't help them at least don't hurt them. The best possible life you can have is one of helping others, and constantly striving to do what is right, regardless of the outcome.

How do you know what is right? Search your heart. Buddha is about compassion; Jesus is about love. Put those together and it's pretty powerful. Treat everyone with dignity, respect, love, and compassion. The reward you receive is the knowledge and peace of mind that you did what was right.

I spent a career in the US Army continually taking and giving orders, and telling soldiers what to do. I came to an understanding that I could not control events. All I could do was try to lead a good life, help others, and set a positive example. I have failed over and over again. My joy comes from helping others when I can, and watching my children excel and lead good lives.

Now to the subject of my novels.

Writing the books *Sparrow's Tears, Close Your Eyes and See, Timeless Terror, Timeless Soldier, Timeless Embrace,* and *Timeless Destiny* became therapy for me — the best therapy. When I think of my son James, I see him always helping others — those who could not help themselves — whether at home or in school. He made me realize that nothing is without purpose; that there is a majestic plan which unfolds itself across the vastness of time equally embracing each life, no more or less important than another. Writing the novels became my way of honoring and paying tribute to James. It allowed me to envision him as an adult, giving him the type of life I would have wished for him. Writing the books allowed me to dream my son a life which I felt had ended too quickly. James Cenney is alive in the pages of my novels. He encourages my readers and me to move forever forward in life.

The hero of my novels — Captain James Ross — is patterned after my son. They both have the same looks, style, loves, and ambience. They are both heroes. But even more than that, as my son James Cenney would say, they "... are intelligent human beings."

My fervent hope is that veterans who are suffering from PTSD and depression can use fiction writing as therapy.

Bernard Cenney
Floresville, Texas

TIMELESS TERROR

PART ONE

I have seen enough of one war never to wish to see another.

Thomas Jefferson
1743 — 1826
3rd US President

PROLOGUE

CHRISTMAS EVE 1944

It's a cold night.

Large flakes of glistening white snow were gently falling and swirling around him.

The playful flakes encircled him, and merged with the rest of the frosty winter wonderland at his feet.

The soldier was uncomfortable, and stomped his feet on the frozen ground.

My God it's cold, he thought to himself.

Unbuttoning a pocket on his tunic, he slid his hand in and automatically extracted a cigarette lighter.

He popped open the top and flicked the thumbwheel downward. The welcome spark ignited a wavering blue flame.

Holding the lighter flame to the cigarette between his lips, the soldier cocked his head to the side and allowed himself the luxury of a long, slow draw.

He held the smoke in his lungs for a moment, and then snapped the little top back down on the lighter.

Tilting his head upwards, the soldier hissed the tobacco vapors out through his nostrils.

He glanced down at the small silver lighter in the palm of his hand.

The weathered cigarette lighter was emblazoned with the unit crest of the Second SS Panzer Division Das Reich.

Otto Skorzeny rubbed his thumb over the crest and smiled.

I have been colder.

Yes, he thought, *the Eastern Front in '41 was much colder.*

Back then, he had been assigned to the Second SS Panzer Division during the Battle of Moscow.

That was extraordinarily cold!

But Otto Skorzeny escaped Russia alive in December 1942 after receiving shrapnel wounds in the back of his head from a Soviet artillery rocket.

Well, that was nothing a little aspirin and schnapps couldn't cure.

He took another drag on his cigarette.

Now he was getting cold *and* restless.

He knew the Third Reich was falling apart, and he was determined to give every last ounce of his strength and courage to the cause.

He was determined to do whatever was necessary to fight on until the inevitable end.

He was determined to survive the war.

The humiliating defeat of Germany in the First World War had created a devastating economic depression that millions of families, including his own, had to endure.

But now, he had prestige and authority.

The Nazis had given him that.

Hell, I earned that. Wasn't I the Führer's chief commando?

Skorzeny looked down at his black Waffen-SS uniform decked out with all its regalia. The Knight's Cross Medal with Oak Leaves Cluster was chaffing at his neck, so he reached up and pulled it off. He shoved the medal into his trousers pocket.

The Waffen-SS, or Schutzstaffel, was the Protective Squadron of the Nazi Party. But their role had increased as the war had grown. Now they had been expanded to thirty-eight divisions, and fought right alongside the Heer, which was the regular German army. The SS had not been totally integrated into the regular army, because they were supposed to become an elite police force after Germany had won the war.

Slim chance of that happening now, he thought.

At six feet four inches tall, and with a seven inch fencer's dueling scar across the left side of his face, all two hundred pounds of Otto Skorzeny were lean, hard, and menacingly formidable. His eyes were light brown, and close friends swore that they saw them twinkle at times. Crows' feet crept from the corners of his eyes, and his eyebrows were dark, long, and wispy. His large ears looked like they had been smashed and flattened by the treads of a Russian tank. His full head of dark brown hair was combed straight back, and he sported a small aristocratic mustache.

Achieving the rank of Obersturmbannführer was an honor for him. As a Lieutenant Colonel in the Waffen-SS, he expected to be given responsible assignments worthy of his grade and experience. Personal daring and audacity had been his operational trademarks. Skorzeny became Hitler's favorite commando after his brilliant rescue of Italian dictator Benito Mussolini on the twelfth of September 1943.

But like the Chinese say, "Be careful of what you wish for. You may just get it."

So for months now, he had been selecting agents for the behind-the-lines Nazi plan known as Operation WERWOLF. These specialized teams, personally trained by him, would conduct sabotage and guerrilla operations after the Third Reich disintegrated.

Recently, he had also been chosen as the Commander of Operation GREIF. That clandestine mission involved German soldiers disguised in US Army uniforms, penetrating behind the lines, to create havoc and confusion during the Ardennes Offensive.

Since August however, the Führer had ordered him to secure certain documents and precious treasures of the Reich, in order to safeguard them against falling into the hands of the Allies.

Hitler believed in the scorched earth policy — the total destruction of Germany. Skorzeny believed in survival and tomorrow.

That's why he organized the WERWOLF Teams to provide cover support for the escape and evasion organization of former SS members, more operationally known by its abbreviation as ODESSA.

We've got to ensure those exit ratlines stay open.

Skorzeny realized that ODESSA would need immense funding in order to facilitate the means to clandestinely egress soldiers out of Germany.

Some of the riches he purposely submerged at Lake Toplitz in the Salzkammergut district; surviving Nazi divers were tasked to recover them after the war. Other loot he secretly buried in the canyon walls of the Totes Gebirge Mountains.

One item he hid in a mountain mine shaft was the highly classified device known simply by its codename — Die Glocke.

The device was about the size of a sedan, only resembling a large bell. The German words *Die Glocke* translate to *The Bell* in English. In the race to beat the Allies from creating an atomic bomb, Die Glocke was a machine that stabilized fissionable materials as a controllable energy source. The ultimate aim was to create atomic weapons. The secondary goal was to generate gyroscopically controlled atomic power to propel advanced aircraft designs. It was one of the Führer's wonder weapons, designed to guarantee total victory.

Atomic bombs or supersonic jet planes, whatever would help us win this damn war, thought Skorzeny.

But there was another rumor about Die Glocke circulating through the ranks of the Schutzstaffel.

Some in the SS said the machine had another purpose.

Some said it involved sorcery.

Some said it involved looking at the past, and seeing into the future.

Some whispered that Die Glocke was a machine for traveling through time itself.

Utter nonsense, thought Skorzeny.

Witches and demons!

Broomsticks and spells!

Mumbo-jumbo!

What children they are, thought Skorzeny.

He hoped Die Glocke would create an atomic weapon for the Fatherland which could be used immediately to win the war.

His thoughts drifted off to his beloved Fatherland.

Ah, for just one more season in the forests of the Salzkammergut!

To be able to go hunting!

To spend one more summer at Lake Toplitz!

But Skorzeny realized those were wishful thoughts.

Tonight, he was in Geneva at the Swiss National Bank, making the last of three deposits of war-spoils gold bars procured from the Berlin Reichsbank. He had already placed equivalent funds in bank depositories in Zurich and Basel.

Skorzeny had convoyed, from Germany to Switzerland, nearly twenty-five tons of gold in the past month.

With the Reichsmark losing its value long ago, the Wehrmacht now calculated the total worth of the pilfered gold in American dollars only.

Skorzeny did a little calculating of his own in his mind.

Now let's see. The US Army is currently valuing gold at thirty-five American dollars per ounce. So, sixteen ounces in a pound, and two thousand pounds in a ton ...

Hmmmmm ...

At twenty-five tons, that is roughly twenty-eight million American dollars.

Skorzeny smiled.

That should keep the escape and evasion pipelines open for a while, he thought.

The gold deposits were secured to three branch offices of the Swiss National Bank: one in Zurich, one in Basel, and this one in Geneva. They each had a separate account number.

A copy of all the account numbers was in the file which Skorzeny had placed in a safety deposit box, along with signatory authority, allowing the owner of the box unbridled access to all the accounts. The key to the safety deposit box hung around Skorzeny's thick Viennese neck.

Skorzeny took another long, slow draw on his cigarette.

Six Waffen-SS soldiers from his command were wheeling the gold bullion ingots into the bank on steel dollies. Two other uniformed Storm Troopers with Sturmgewehr model 44 assault rifles stood guard alongside Skorzeny.

The work was laborious, but it was nearly done.

After waiting for the last of the gold to be hauled in, Skorzeny pointed with his index finger, directing his SS guards to enter the vestibule of the bank.

With a flick of his fingers, Skorzeny sent what was left of his cigarette flying off like a tiny sputtering meteorite, drilling its way into the sludge of a nearby snow bank.

Taking a quick glance skyward at the gently falling snow, Skorzeny lowered his head while hunching up his shoulders, and followed his men inside the bank.

The warmth of the bank interior pleasantly reassured him.

Finally out of the damn cold, he thought.

The lobby of the Swiss National Bank was nothing short of extravagant opulence. The chiseled blue-gray marble floor flowed out like a vast glimmering ocean, from which the *"clip-clop, clip-clop"* sound of receptionist shoes echoed forth. Towering Nordic-style pillars twisted and turned their way upward, supporting a ceiling resplendent with scenes from Norse mythology.

The ceiling was completely domed, and had been hand-painted with elaborate frescoes of the Norse Gods. In the center was a celestial sky scene with Odin, King of the Norse Gods, and the father of battle. On the right was a magnificent underwater scene filled with sea serpents and nymphs, depicting the world of Aegir, the Norse God of the Seas. On the left side was an erotica scene with a beautiful Goddess holding the hands of a nude man and woman.

Skorzeny thought for a moment.

Who is that supposed to be?

Then it came to him.

Of course!

That's Lofn, the comforter!

She's the Goddess and arranger of marriages and unions ...

Skorzeny then realized the irony of desperate soldiers depositing plundered gold in a neutral Swiss bank.

... even arranging forbidden unions!

Three majestic crystal chandeliers hanging from the ceiling added a mystic illumination to the already otherworldly scene.

An expanse of exquisitely hand-varnished dark brown mahogany counters loomed at Skorzeny and his guards as they made their way across the foyer.

The portly bank director saw Skorzeny step inside and immediately scuttled over to intercept him.

Champagne materialized with a snap of the bank director's fingers. It was ushered over on trays to the Lieutenant Colonel and his men by three gorgeous blonde female receptionists.

Like the Valkyries, carrying us to Valhalla.

Skorzeny motioned to his troops with his hands, beckoning them to gather around him and the champagne-laden Aryan women.

"Men, go ahead and help yourselves to some drink," ordered the Obersturmbannführer.

His soldiers all reached over and picked up dainty crystal glasses bubbling with champagne and waited.

Skorzeny reached down and delicately picked up a glass of frothing champagne in his calloused hands.

Hitler's top commando looked at his Wehrmacht issued Phenix wristwatch. Its luminous blade-type hands revealed to him that it was just three minutes before midnight.

Nearly midnight. My God it's almost Christmas day.

Raising his glass to Valhalla, the now grinning Otto Skorzeny bellowed, "Men, Merry Christmas to you all!"

The smiling soldiers all raised their glasses and thundered back in unison, "Merry Christmas, sir!"

The soldiers drank everything in very deeply. They didn't know how much longer such luxuries as pretty women, champagne, or even the warmth from a fire would be available to them.

Skorzeny put down his empty glass and said, "That will be all men. Please wait for me outside."

As his Storm Troopers filed past, Skorzeny held out his hand saying, "Not you, Obersturmführer Lugoff. You come with me."

Turning his gaze to the bank director, Skorzeny said, "Let's finalize our paperwork, Herr Director."

The portly bank director bowed and then led Skorzeny and his Lieutenant into his most private of offices.

"Please sit down gentlemen," said the bank director motioning to the two chairs in front of his desk.

The Lieutenant stood obediently and waited for his commander to take his seat first.

SS-Obersturmführer Wilhelm von Lugoff had been Skorzeny's executive officer now for the past five months. Lugoff had served the Third Reich in some capacity or other since before his fifteenth birthday. His current rank of SS-Obersturmführer had been earned, along with his Knight's Cross Medal, at the Siege of Sevastopol.

Lugoff was born in the seaport town of Bremerhaven. He had been raised in a privileged upper class Germanic disciplinarian family. Like most Germans, his father had also been a soldier, serving in the First World War as a Captain in the Imperial German Army. His father had been killed in the 1918 Battle of the Marne, and so Wilhelm naturally followed the footsteps of his father into the military.

Now at twenty-six years of age, Lugoff's youthful boyish appearance concealed his efficient military ruthlessness.

His dark brown hair was combed to the right side, and was rather long for a soldier. His thin, brown, over-arching eyebrows seemed to resemble quotation marks on his forehead whenever he smiled. His jade green hued eyes were strikingly vivid and clear. He had high cheek bones and a slender aristocratic nose, below which sat thin and always smiling lips. His natural good looks, charisma, and politeness were considered cute by the young Frauleins. With a slender build and standing six feet two inches tall, he was still two inches shorter than Skorzeny.

The bank director lowered his head and carefully studied the document on the desk in front of him. Seemingly satisfied, he raised his head and smiled.

Peering through the wire-rimmed glasses perched on his nose, the bank director looked at Skorzeny and said, "Everything seems to be in order here, mein Herr. All that is required is your signature."

The bank director turned the document around and placed it in the center of his desk. He gently extracted a fountain pen from its holder and held it out for Skorzeny.

"There's been a slight change of plans Herr Director," said Skorzeny menacingly. "Both I and my Lieutenant will sign the document jointly now."

The bank director unexpectedly dropped the fountain pen on his desk, and then rapidly recovered it. His nervous eyes shifted quickly from Skorzeny to Lugoff.

"But of course mein Herr. Of course. That will not be a problem," said the rattled bank director. "Herr Lugoff may place his signature directly next to yours. Then you will both have custody jointly, mein Herr."

Skorzeny smiled. He grasped the proffered fountain pen and scratched his signature onto the parchment paper.

"Sign next to me, Wilhelm," said Skorzeny, handing him the pen.

Lugoff took the fountain pen and carefully inscribed his name and rank next to his commanding officer.

The bank director then methodically blotted the signatures with a Mont Blanc rubber block.

"Very good gentlemen," said the bank director. "This original document will be processed and safeguarded here at our facility." He pressed the switch on his desk intercom and spoke gently into the small mahogany box.

"Please come in here, Irma. I need you to Photostat a document immediately. Thank you my dear," said the bank director.

"Gentlemen, my secretary Irma will copy this document for you. It will take about five minutes with our Photostat machine. Is there anything else I can do for you now?" asked the bank director.

Skorzeny looked at Lugoff.

"Perhaps some more of your exquisite champagne while we wait, Herr Director," said Skorzeny.

"Yes of course. Please follow me gentlemen."

All three men rose up, and then the bank director nervously led them out of his private office and back into the lobby of the Swiss National Bank.

"Excuse me gentlemen while I arrange for the refreshments."

Once the bank director had gone, Skorzeny stepped close to Lugoff and spoke quietly.

"I wanted to add you as joint owner of this account," said Skorzeny, "just in case anything happens to me."

Lugoff said, "Nothing is going to happen to you, sir."

Skorzeny waved his hand dismissively in front of him and said, "Be that as it may, I want you to survive this war and swear to me you will use these accounts to continue our struggle."

Lugoff straightened up and replied, “Why yes sir. I will sir. It will be my honor, sir.”

Skozeny smiled.

“I know it will, Wilhelm. I have the utmost trust in your abilities. These funds will secure a future for our survivors after the war. It will buy freedom to begin with.”

Skorzeny then scanned around the bank to make sure they were out of earshot of anyone.

“And when the time is right, my dear Wilhelm, these funds may be just the catalyst to ensure a future victory.”

Skorzeny reached up and lifted the cord with the safety deposit box key from around his own neck. He pressed the key into Lugoff’s hand.

“Here is the key to the safety deposit box which contains all the account numbers and documentation. Take care of it. I entrust it to you. It’s safer around your neck than mine.”

Lugoff slipped the cord with the key over his head and around his neck. He tucked it inside his shirt so the key was hidden from view.

“It will never leave me, sir,” said Lugoff.

Skorzeny patted Lugoff on the back, as a father would his son.

“I know, Wilhelm,” said Skorzeny.

By this time, the bank director had sent three female receptionists scurrying over to the two Nazi officers. One had a tray with champagne, while the other women had trays filled with various tidbits and finger food delicacies.

Skorzeny and Lugoff each picked up a goblet of champagne.

"Wilhelm, I don't know how I could have accomplished this mission so efficiently without your planning expertise," said Skorzeny.

Beaming a big toothy smile, Lugoff replied, "Thank you sir. Serving with you these past months has been the greatest honor of my life."

By now the bank director had rejoined the three women standing around the two officers. Unexpectedly, Skorzeny stepped back and raised his right arm in the Nazi salute.

"One people, one Reich, one Führer!" said Skorzeny triumphantly.

The bank director was clearly startled.

Lugoff returned the victory salute and responded with a vigorous, "Sieg Heil!"

Now the bank director was trembling.

The stares of both Nazi officers bored into the bank director's skull. His quivering lips finally opened.

"Ah, yes of course mein Herr."

Raising his right palm while clearing his throat, the bank director squeaked out the most abhorrent of all words to him.

"Ah-hem — yes — Heil — Heil Hitler."

PRESENT DAY

In war, truth is the first casualty.

Aeschylus
525 — 456 BC
Ancient Greek Playwright

CHAPTER ONE

WATER BREAKS ROCK

Helmand Province is one of the thirty-four provinces found in Afghanistan. Located in southern Afghanistan, Helmand is one of the largest provinces, with over a thousand villages and well over a million people. Helmand is also the major opium producing region in Afghanistan, responsible for seventy-five per cent of the world's production.

Lashkar Gah is the capital of Helmand. With a population of just over two hundred thousand, Lashkar Gah is serviced by the Bost Airport.

Originally built in 1957 with United States funding, Bost Airport now has the third longest runway in Afghanistan, and several newly renovated terminal buildings.

Located behind the control tower and just opposite the restaurant is a terminal building known only by its number: #23. Building #23 is an innocent looking cinder block structure, two stories high, and sporting a roof festooned with antennas. Armed personnel stand guard at its entrance, and the building is surrounded on three sides by revetments.

Revetments — in military lingo — are blast protective walls.

Building #23 is a busy place, with people going in and coming out at all hours.

People speak in hushed tones about Building #23.

Some say it is a gathering place for spies.

Others say it is a command center.

Some even say it is a prison.

Still others say people go in and never come out.

Currently the building located behind the control tower and just opposite the restaurant, known only by the number "23" stenciled in black paint above its front door, is an active Central Intelligence Agency safe house.

Operationally, Building #23 houses an interrogation chamber for prisoners.

The standard of international law for the acceptable humanitarian treatment of prisoners of war was established long ago by the Geneva Conventions. In diplomacy, the term *convention* means *international agreement.* The 1949 Geneva Convention, relative to the treatment of prisoners of war, does not apply to terrorists however. The Geneva Convention only applies to international conflicts between nation-states or countries that have signed on accepting the agreements.

Al-Qaeda is not a nation-state or country.

Since Afghanistan had signed the Geneva treaties, the Taliban fighters originally had somewhat of a claim to the protection of the Conventions. To maintain a humanitarian prisoner of war or POW status, signatories must follow the Geneva protocols. These protocols consist of guidelines for combatants such as: wearing a recognizable military uniform, obeying the laws and customs of warfare, and not deliberately targeting civilians.

The Taliban lost its protected status when it refused to follow the Geneva protocols.

Therefore, al-Qaeda and Taliban detainees, or prisoners, are not governed under the Geneva Convention rules.

This does not mean that al-Qaeda and Taliban prisoners are not treated humanely. They are. But it does mean, however, that they are allowed to be psychologically finessed into giving up information. Sometimes that finessing happens from a rag and a bucket of water.

Today, Jennie Nelson was conducting the questioning of a detainee.

Jennie Nelson was an athletic looking twenty-nine year old woman. She had dark brown hair, cut short and parted in the middle. Her eyebrows were thin, and elegantly accented her sky blue eyes. She had European features with a small straight nose, high cheek bones, full lips, and a slightly pointed chin.

Jennie rarely wore makeup, except for the clear wet-looking lip gloss she had on today. She was wearing round, brilliant-cut, glittering, quarter carat cubic zirconia gemstones in her ear lobes. She always kept her unpainted fingernails cut short, and her palms usually had calluses from overindulgence in weightlifting. Her left wrist was adorned with a stainless steel Rolex Yacht-Master chronometer. She wore no rings on her fingers.

Jennie was well known and loved for always wearing skirts, with today being no exception.

She was wearing a white cotton blouse and a knee-length khaki skirt that was enticingly stretched taut across her muscular buttocks. A three inch wide black belt with a large silver buckle held the ensemble together. Jennie's legs were long, tan, and sexy, with muscled calves that teased you into wanting to run your hands over them. Her feet were nestled into shiny black pumps with a three inch heel.

Jennie was beautiful, and knew she was beautiful. She considered herself a professional intelligence officer, and avoided flirting at all costs. She knew it didn't hurt to be good looking though.

Originally from Minot North Dakota, Jennie attended Georgetown University and graduated with a bachelor degree in Middle Eastern Studies, with a minor in Farsi. Upon graduation, she was eagerly recruited by the Central Intelligence Agency and was assigned as a basic Intelligence Collection Analyst.

After proving herself linguistically, promotions came rather quickly. She applied and was selected to attend the Armed Forces Experimental Training Activity at Camp Peary in Williamsburg, Virginia. Ever the achiever, Jennie graduated in the top five percent of her class from the Basic Operations Course. That was followed by SERE, or Survival Evasion Resistance and Escape, training at Fort Bragg. Before she knew it, Jennie was offered a Case Officer position in Afghanistan.

This morning at the Bost Airport in Building #23, Jennie was observing two of her burly assistants hold down a shackled thirty-five year old prisoner by the name of Abu Bari al-Rahman. A third man, whom Jennie only knew as *Frank the contractor,* was holding what looked like a centuries-old red colored rag over al-Rahman's face, and systematically pouring pitchers of water through the cloth and into his nose and mouth.

This was what the media referred to as *waterboarding.*

Abu Bari al-Rahman was a member of al-Qaeda.

Al-Qaeda, in the Arabic language, literally means *the Base*. It was the name given to training camps of the Mujahedeen. The Mujahedeen were Muslim guerrillas in the fight against the invading Soviet Army in the 1980s.

Back then, these Afghan freedom fighters were supported by the United States government. They were conducting Jihad, or a Holy War, against the Soviet invaders.

Today, the remnants of the Mujahedeen conduct Jihad against the United States, which they also see as invaders. They believe the Christian West is trying to destroy the Islamic East.

Abu Bari al-Rahman was a member of the money committee of al-Qaeda, which originally operated out of Abbottabad Pakistan. He operated through the Hawala banking system, which was basically similar to money brokers. Al-Rahman's job was to receive funds and launder them to avoid any trace of where they originated from.

The questioning was going very well today.

"Okay Abu, tell me once more, where did the money come from for the explosives?" said Frank.

Gasping for breath, al-Rahman whispered, "From the professor."

"Nice. Okay Abu, and who is the professor?"

Al-Rahman hung his head down.

Frank looked exasperated.

"Do you want another swimming lesson, Abby?"

Al-Rahman raised his head feebly and shook it slowly back and forth.

"I'll ask you one more time. Who is the professor?" patiently asked Frank.

Al-Rahman slowly lowered his head.

"Okay pal, here we go again," said Frank.

Frank nodded affirmatively to his two assistant interrogators.

The men positioned themselves on either side of the detainee, and each pressed a knee down hard on the prisoners' shoulders. One man aggressively pushed down and held al-Rahman's head steady on the bench.

Frank picked up the pitcher of cold water and brought it into al-Rahman's field of vision.

Al-Rahman trembled and began pleading with Frank.

"Wait, wait please!" implored al-Rahman in piteous supplication.

Frank held up the palm of his hand, signaling for his assistants to ease up.

"What do you have for me, Abby?" asked Frank.

Gasping for breath, al-Rahman said, "The professor is one of you."

Jennie's interest was piqued at al-Rahman's response, so she walked over and stood directly next to Frank.

Frank was used to prisoners saying anything until they broke. And everyman broke, sooner or later. He had learned over the years to be a patient man.

"What do you mean — one of us?" asked Frank.

Al-Rahman whispered, “He’s USA government.”

“What?” Frank asked.

Al-Rahman said, “He’s educated.”

Frank explored further.

“How is he educated?”

Al-Rahman said, “He’s a teacher.”

Frank felt like he was talking to a stalling child.

“Okay. What kind of teacher? Is he an actual college professor?”

Al-Rahman realized his options were running out. He knew this American, known as Frank, would continue with the simulated drowning all week, day after day.

Al-Rahman said, “Yes. He teaches at a university in Switzerland.”

Frank asked, “What else?”

Al-Rahman said, “He is one of you, but he is also a ghost.”

“What do you mean — a ghost?” asked Frank mimicking al-Rahman’s tone.

Al-Rahman whispered, “He is of the past.”

Frank became intrigued. He had his assistants sit al-Rahman up on the bench.

Now we’re getting somewhere.

“What do you mean — of the past?” asked Frank.

Al-Rahman studied Frank’s face for a moment.

“He is of the past, the past wars. The professor is of the crooked-cross,” said al-Rahman.

Frank looked at al-Rahman with a puzzled expression.

Al-Rahman said, “You know, the Germans, Hitler, and World War Two.”

Frank looked at both of his assistants who shook their heads negatively.

"How can that be?" demanded Frank.

Al-Rahman said, "The professor provides us funding. We use his monies for arms and supplies. The money is untraceable."

Frank asked, "How is it untraceable?"

Al-Rahman said, "Because it is gold."

Now Jennie spoke up for the first time.

"The professor pays you in gold?" exclaimed Jennie.

Al-Rahman nodded his head up and down.

"Yes. Only a few paymasters from the money committee have actually seen the gold. I am one who has seen."

"And?" interjected Jennie.

"I have seen the gold. It is not coin, but bars of gold. They are stamped with the German symbol."

Jennie asked, "You mean a cross, a German cross?"

Al-Rahman nodded his head up and down.

"Yes, the German cross. But an eagle sits atop this cross. The cross is crooked on the ends."

Jennie looked at Frank, and then back to al-Rahman.

She walked over to Frank's small wooden desk and picked up a paper and pencil.

Jennie walked back and handed the paper and pencil to the prisoner.

"Draw it for me," said Jennie.

Al-Rahman took the pencil and very carefully sketched a symbol on the paper.

“There,” said al-Rahman. “Like that.”

Jennie and Frank peered over and looked at the piece of paper.

Al-Rahman had very neatly drawn a symbol of Germany.

There was no mistake.

It was right there on the paper, clear as day.

Only the emblem was of an older Germany.

It was a badge of a past Germany.

It was a stamp of an evil Germany.

The symbol was the sinister Nazi Swastika.

CHAPTER TWO

DEATH TOLL

It was just after midnight.

A time referred to as the witches' hour.

Lin Sparrow tossed and turned in her bed.

Sweat was beading on her forehead.

A low guttural moaning noise emanated from her throat and pushed through her lips.

Lin was asleep and dreaming.

It was the identical dream, night after night —

— night after night.

The dream always started the same way.

It was long ago, in the distant past.

A past that was violent and shrouded in the misery of war.

Winter was yawning, and the air was frigid and crisp.

Snow covered the ground, and icicles hung from evergreen tree branches like glittering tinsel.

It was twilight — that time when the sun has just set, and the earth is neither completely lit nor completely dark.

Christmas Eve had arrived.

Armed German soldiers, from a war long lost, were marching a winding column of prisoners on a road to a new camp.

The column was enshrouded with the frozen puffs of breath searing out of the throats of the prisoners.

The road was blackened by a mixture of churned up sludge from constant campaigns, and the soot of a thousand diesel engines.

They were in southern Germany, and close to the Swiss border.

The Swiss Alps could be seen through the hazy curtain of winter.

The road turned by a lake — a lake frozen from sub-zero temperatures.

A German officer stopped marching and pointed towards the lake. He barked out a hideously sinister order to one of his soldiers.

The SS-Sturmmann soldier looked at the officer incredulously, and then obeyed. He turned towards the column of human flesh and grabbed a ten year old Jewish girl by the arm. He began dragging the little girl towards the lake.

The young Jewish girl went limp and started to sob uncontrollably as the German soldier dragged her about fifty feet out onto the frozen surface of the lake.

The soldier released his grip on the arm of the girl, and then violently pushed her forward. He cautiously crept back across the surface of the lake to the road, making sure his carefully placed footsteps did not crack the ice asunder.

The German officer sauntered across to the point at which the ground buttressed the frozen lake.

The German was smiling now as he unsnapped the flap of his belt holster and slowly drew out his model P-08 nine millimeter Mauser pistol.

The officer held the Mauser with his right hand, and extended his arm forward in the classic pistol dueling mode.

An American prisoner of war, Army Captain James Ross, brushed with his left hand at the shock of brown hair that always fell across his forehead. It stayed put for a second, then just fell back down again. He watched in horror as the Schutzstaffel officer methodically took aim at the ice under the feet of the little girl.

BAM!

The first shot pierced the ice, but did little damage.

Both hands of the startled Jewish girl went up to her mouth, and she began uncontrollably trembling in abject fear.

BAM!

The second bullet came closer to the feet of the little girl, and made her cry out.

"Help me!"

"Please!"

"Mama, Papa!"

"Please!"

"Help me God!"

The Schutzstaffel German officer laughed out loud.

"This Jew bitch is crying to her God!" he yelled to the column of prisoners.

"Ah ha, ha, ha, ha, ha!"

Now, the German officer grasped the Mauser in both hands and steadied his aim.

BAM!

His third shot pierced the ice so close to the startled little girl that she fell over and her body impact cracked the icy surface.

Slowly, very slowly, the face of the glittering lake underneath the young girl started to shatter and collapse.

With a *"splash"* the girl crashed through the ice and frenziedly reached up, groping for a handhold.

The American prisoner had had enough.

Captain Ross broke ranks and walked away from the column of prisoners and towards the little Jewish girl in the frozen lake waters.

The German officer became startled as the American officer brushed past him.

"Achtung!" yelled the Nazi officer.

The American Captain kept walking forward towards the girl.

The Nazi officer became angry.

"Anhalten!" screamed the German.

The American officer said viciously, "Go to hell."

Now the German officer leveled his Mauser pistol at the back of the American soldier.

"Stop now, Amerikaner," yelled the German while aiming his pistol.

The American Captain was now on the surface of the lake and about twenty feet from the thrashing little girl.

BAM!

A nine millimeter bullet slapped into his right shoulder.

The American Captain let out a grunt of pain, but kept walking forward to help the struggling girl. The Nazi officer became enraged. He steadied his aim and shot again.

BAM!

This fifth bullet tore into the prisoner's right thigh.

Collapsing to the icy surface, the American Captain now began crawling towards the young Jewish girl.

Finally, the American soldier reached the little girl. He slid his arms forward and plunged them into the icy waters.

The Jewish girl frantically grabbed his hands, and the American started to pull her out of her icy hell.

Fully irate now, the German officer began gingerly walking across the surface of the lake to the scene.

With all the strength she could muster, the little Jewish girl pulled herself out of the frigid waters by clawing and climbing onto the back of the American soldier.

"You'll be all right now, darling," said the American Captain reassuringly smiling.

Sliding his body around on the icy surface and away from the shattered hole, the American Captain got to his knees and started crawling back towards shore.

The entire prisoner of war column had halted by this time, and was watching the eerie scene unfold.

German guards armed with Sturmgewehr assault rifles stood by, not knowing exactly what to do next.

Leaving a crimson metallic-smelling blood trail, the American Captain had crawled with the little girl on his back about twenty-five feet now. He figured that was a safe enough distance away from the icy opening to try and stand up. Slowly, painfully, agonizingly, the American Captain brought his knees up to his chest first, and then straightened his arms to push himself up.

But his hands slipped in his own blood, and he came crashing down hard onto the ice once again.

Methodically pushing down using his knees as support, the Captain wobbly straightened his legs and struggled to his feet with the Jewish girl clinging to his back.

With a pool of vermilion blood beneath him, the Captain leaned forward and began to stagger towards the shore.

By this time, the German officer was only about seven or eight feet away. He stopped and pointed his Mauser at the desperate pair.

"Herr Hauptmann Ross, you have come as far as you are going to go," said the gleeful Nazi.

The American Captain looked at the Nazi and said, "You're pretty good terrorizing children, Kraut. How are you when they come a little bigger?"

Frustration showed on the face of the Nazi officer.

"Enough!" he yelled.

BAM!

The bullet tore through the chest of the American Captain and exited the back of the little Jewish girl clinging to him.

Both were killed instantly.

The American soldier and the young girl crumpled to the surface and shattered the ice below them.

The Nazi officer stared in horror as the frigid surface disintegrated before his eyes into a thousand pieces, and all three of them sank into the abyss of the frozen lake waters.

Deeper and deeper the trio descended into an icy, watery grave.

Clang!

The column of prisoners slowly turned their heads to gaze at a church steeple.

Hanging in the steeple was a bell.

It was bigger than a man, about the size of a small automobile.

The bell was illuminated and glowing greenish-orange this time.

The bell resumed tolling.

Clang!

Clang!

Clang!

The bell was ringing a toll of death.

Noooooooooooo!

Lin Sparrow awoke at six o'clock in the morning with the jolt of an electric spark.

Her nude body was glistening from head to toe with trickles of cold sweat.

She kicked off the thin white bed sheet that had been covering her, and walked slowly into the small bathroom of her apartment.

Lin clicked on the lights and examined her face in the large mirror hanging above the ancient porcelain sink.

This is crazy.

I've had the same dream, over and over now, for weeks.

Something is up.

Something is going to happen to James.

I can see it.

I can feel it.

I know it.

My mother said I was a seer.

My father said I had the gift.

I've always had it.

Back home, our neighbors called it witchcraft.

Others called it clairvoyance.

Whatever its name — I've got it.

I've got to do something.

I've got to find James before it's too late, she thought.

Then Lin started to rationalize.

She knew these dreams were more than nightmares or visions; they were memories.

She stared deeply into the brown eyes analyzing her in the mirror.

I've got two weeks of Christmas leave coming from my nursing job.

I'll take them both.

But where will I go?

Lin stared back at herself in the mirror.

You know where, don't you?

You know exactly where to go.

Switzerland, she told herself.

It's always been Switzerland.

The signs have all been pointing to Switzerland.

Switzerland.

Switzerland.

Switzerland.

Lin picked up her tube of minty Crest toothpaste and squeezed a dab out onto her pink toothbrush. She brushed her teeth quickly, and then gargled with an antiseptic mouthwash, and spat out the residue in the sink.

She walked over to the shower stall and slid open the transparent glass door, stepped inside, and then closed the door behind her.

With hot water jets pulsating, Lin scrubbed herself in the steamy shower with lavender deep moisturizing body wash, and lathered her hair with strawberry Garnier Fructis shampoo.

Lin thoroughly rinsed herself with tepid water, and then stepped out of the shower. She grabbed a large red terrycloth towel and dried herself off.

She walked over to her teakwood dresser and creaked open the drawer.

Lin put on a sheer pair of panties and matching bra. Then she selected a black silk knee-length skirt and a light blue blouse. She slipped a two baht gold chain, with matching Buddha, around her neck, and strapped a stainless steel Citizen Eco-Drive ProMaster Diver watch with black rubber band onto her left wrist. She splashed Organza Indecence perfume on her neck, and rubbed her wrists together with a dash.

Lin looked at herself in the timeworn bathroom mirror.

She was five feet nine inches tall.

That was tall for a Malaysian lady.

But Lin was only half Malay.

She was a mixture of East and West, just like her American boyfriend, Captain James Ross.

Lin's mother, Mira Wan Tengku, was Malay, and her father, Lieutenant Alastair Jasper Sparrow, had been a British Special Air Service officer assigned to their embassy at Kuala Lumpur. He had been killed from a terrorist bomb explosion when Lin was just a child. She had never really gotten to know her father all that well. Her mother never remarried, and had kept the last name of Sparrow. Lin was twenty-five years old now.

She continued staring at herself in the mirror.

Her silky raven locks cascaded slightly below her shoulders, with bangs that stopped just above her eyebrows. She had long eyelashes, and a petite nose that was slightly upturned. Her eyes were deep brown almonds that sparkled in the light, and her mouth was large and femininely beautiful, with glistening full lips. Her skin was very smooth with almost no body hair. She kept her fingernails cut short and unpainted; however she did apply a clear polish to her toenails.

Lin reached down and picked up a cosmetic brush to apply a small trace of rouge blush powder to her Western cheeks.

When she was done, she looked around and slipped her feet into well worn, ebony, three inch heeled pumps.

Lin was extremely troubled by her dreams about her boyfriend James Ross. She knew he was in mortal danger. She knew she had to get to Switzerland.

Switzerland has been present in all my dreams about James, thought Lin.

But I have a friend in Switzerland, don't I? I have an ally.

I know that my old boss, Mister Watlington, retired from the Foreign Service and is now teaching college in Zurich. I could email him and tell him I'm coming to Switzerland on vacation, and that maybe we could meet up for a lunch or something. I'll ask him if he can recommend a good hotel for me to stay in.

I know Mister Watlington. He's a good man. He'll help me out.

Lin used to serve as Executive Personal Secretary to the Honorable Simon Watlington, the United States Ambassador to Malaysia. That civil service job had been rewarding, but at a cost to her dignity and self-respect. It became just too unbearable for her to work at the US Embassy in Kuala Lumpur anymore. She simply could not stand to work day after day within the labyrinth of backstabbing political machinations.

Lin had always wanted a job that she could be proud of. She wanted to do something that would make a difference in peoples' lives. She wanted to have a sense of actually helping people, of making the world a little better place to live in. She wanted to give something of herself back to the people of Malaysia. Consequently, she enrolled in an accelerated evening studies program at the Puteri Nursing College, and completed her degree. Now she was a critical care registered nurse. She currently worked in the emergency room at the Twin Towers Medical Center, in Kuala Lumpur, Malaysia.

Lin picked up her LG smartphone and emailed Watlington about her Zurich plans.

Then she sent Ross an email, telling him she was going to Zurich.

She couldn't explain her dreams to Ross, just yet. He was much too protective of her. Ross would downplay it, and not want her to come. He would not want to put her in any danger. Ross was just that kind of man.

She finished her email and put her smartphone inside her purse.

Satisfied that she was ready, Lin slung her purple colored purse over her left shoulder. The purse was actually a gift from Ross. It was Texas Christian University purple, and decorated with TCU symbols all over.

Lin walked through her apartment and unlocked the front door. She walked outside and secured the door with a twist of her key, and then lithely scampered down a flight of stairs and out into the bright Kuala Lumpur morning.

The Twin Towers Medical Center is located at the Suria Kuala Lumpur City Center, on Jalan Ampang.

Lin did what she did every morning to get there.

She boarded the Putra Light Rail Transit System, or LRT metro train, which took her from the end of her street to the Ampang Park LRT Station. It usually worked out to be about a fifteen minute ride. Once at the Ampang Park LRT Station, the medical center was only about a ten minute walk.

The LRT was on time today, as it always was. Kuala Lumpur transportation was the epitome of efficiency.

After the fifteen minute ride, Lin exited the Ampang Park Station and walked the small distance to the Twin Towers Medical Center.

Lin had the privilege of working for Doctor Arjinderpal Sekhon. He was considered one of the finest emergency room physicians in all of Kuala Lumpur.

Her mind was occupied with only one thought: getting to James Ross as quickly as possible.

Doctor Sekhon will let me take the two weeks leave, once I tell him everything.

I'll just explain my situation to him.

He'll understand.

He'll support me.

He's a very reasonable man.

CHAPTER THREE

SINS OF THE FATHER

The professor was very carefully choosing his words, and getting ready to end his lecture for the day.

"And so ladies and gentlemen," he smiled, "as we have demonstrated here, one man's terrorist is another man's freedom fighter."

"Are there any questions?"

The professor surveyed his audience.

Seeing no raised hands, he concluded his lecture.

"Very well. Class dismissed."

The professor slowly gathered up his lecture materials and placed them in his satchel.

The University of Zurich is the largest university in Switzerland. The vast, urban campus facilities spread out across Zurich, and support over twenty-five thousand students. No other Swiss university offers a wider range of subjects or degree programs. Founded in 1833, it is ranked in the top ten of all European universities. Nobel Prize Laureate Albert Einstein is one of the University of Zurich's most notable alumni.

The university's Master of Arts in Strategic Studies program is very popular with domestic and international students. This field of study provides students with a comprehensive curriculum of foreign relations, political science, and strategic policy review. Its most popular offering, is a special course in international terrorism.

The University of Zurich's Office of Human Resources considered itself very fortunate to have recently hired a world-renown expert to teach the terrorism course.

That learned professor, teaching the course on international terrorism in Zurich, was none other than the former United States Ambassador to Malaysia — the Honorable Simon Watlington.

For those who first encounter him, Simon Watlington can present a very imposing picture.

Watlington stands at six feet four inches tall. He had been shaving his head to compensate for a receding hairline for years, and now was completely bald. He had thin, brown, over-arching eyebrows that seemed to resemble quotation marks on his forehead whenever he smiled. The left eyebrow was cut in half by a thin scar he received while fencing as a member of the Skull and Bones undergraduate society, decades ago, while at a Yale University competition. His eyes were jade green in color, which caused many people to stare at them unintentionally. He had high cheek bones and a slender aristocratic nose, below which sat thin and always smiling lips. His face was clean shaven, with the smell of musk aftershave.

Watlington was fifty-five years old, and enjoyed staying in shape. His weight hovered monthly between two hundred eighteen, and two hundred and twenty pounds. Exercise was a regular part of his day, and Watlington was considered a master of the Korean martial art of Hwa Rang Do.

Always a man who appreciated the finer things in life, his left wrist was adorned with a Blancpain Fifty Fathoms chronograph timepiece in stainless steel, with a brown crocodile strap. The only ring he wore was a large Master Mason ring, with the square and compass symbols in 18 karat gold, on the third finger of his left hand.

Simon Watlington had resigned from his position and retired from the United States Department of State when the full time professor job had become open at the University of Zurich.

Originally anxious to just retire from his posting in Malaysia and disappear, he quickly changed his mind once the university position was offered.

Switzerland gave him everything that he craved: prestige, power, and protection.

In Switzerland, he could continue his interests and pursuits without restraint.

He could just blend into the scenery anonymously — something that he couldn't do while in the limelight of a Malaysian Ambassadorship.

But then again, very few people in the world knew that he was not really the Honorable Simon Watlington, former United States Ambassador to Malaysia. Over thirty years ago while on a State

Department assignment in Berlin, Simon Watlington had been terribly disfigured in a fiery car crash near Checkpoint Charlie.

That was the official newspaper account anyway.

The real Simon Watlington died in that accident.

That car crash had been planned and prearranged years before.

Simon Watlington had been chosen because he had no siblings, his father and mother were already deceased, and he was a junior Foreign Service Officer whose career could be manipulated.

The Soviet Union's Committee for State Security, better known by its abbreviation as KGB, had chosen and recruited *him* for that task.

The automobile accident scenario had been planned and set up for years in advance by the KGB, intent on having a long-term controllable asset deep inside the United States government.

The real Watlington's body had been switched in the counterfeit ambulance with him, the plastic-surgery-enhanced impostor. He had been beguilingly swathed in bandages and injuries, right down to the facial and vocal cord burns. With the face permanently altered, and the distinct vocal cord changes, who would be the wiser?

Any attempt at positive identification was physically impossible since the fingerprints had been burned off.

Having assumed Watlington's identity, he rotated from position to position in the US State Department throughout the years.

He had become a wolf in sheep's clothing. He was a sleeper agent unbeknownst to all except his handlers — the KGB.

The false Watlington had made it a point, in all of his affairs, to tiptoe through the raindrops.

He was not a naïve man.

He did not see things as black and white.

To Watlington, issues were always gray.

Watlington enjoyed money and power.

He reveled in wielding both to his personal advantage.

He was on the periphery of intricate covert operations that his handlers considered essential.

And he always made sure that the trail never led back to him.

But now was the time for him to collect *his* due.

Now was the time for them to pay *their* bill.

Now he was turning friend against friend, and foe against foe.

He would make the Russians pay, little by little, as he slowly destroyed them with a war.

It was a war as old as time.

It was an asymmetrical war.

It was a guerrilla war.

It was classic unconventional warfare.

And it would never cease.

It would never end.

The Russians are fools, he thought to himself.

They try to control by brute power.

They have no idea of the forces I have mounted against them.

Didn't they destroy my parents?

Didn't they capture my father?

Didn't they torture him?

Didn't they rape my beloved mother?

Didn't they defile her?

Didn't they turn her into their whore?

Those bastards!

I will never forget!

I will never forgive!

Now is the time!

Now is my time!

Didn't I seek out their counsel?

Didn't I allow the Soviets to recruit me?

They thought they could control me!

They thought they could manipulate me out of fear!

It's all part of my plan.

I can't believe how easily they fell into my trap.

The world emptied its barbaric filth on my family.

Now, I will defy the entire world!

I swear to this, just as surely as my father was SS-Obersturmführer Wilhelm von Lugoff!

The counterfeit Watlington took a deep breath and counted to ten.

He remembered back to his past.

He remembered back to his childhood.

It was a childhood filled with fear.

He had been born under a different name.

His real name was Wolfram von Lugoff.

He was the only surviving child of SS-Obersturmführer Wilhelm and Ingrid von Lugoff.

Wilhelm and Ingrid had fallen in love at the beginning of Hitler's reign as Chancellor of Germany. Like all German families at the time, they were encouraged to have as many Aryan offspring as possible to support the Greater Germanic Race. The Lugoff's had been happy to comply, and had four children: Klaus, Dieter, Astrid, and Wolfram.

Ingrid gave birth to Klaus in 1939. Dieter followed in 1941, with Astrid arriving in 1943.

Wolfram's father, Wilhelm, had been a member of the elite SS, or Schutzstaffel. He had served with Hitler's greatest commando, SS-Obersturmbannführer Otto Skorzeny, in the Second SS Panzer Division Das Reich.

Wilhelm had been involved in Operation BARBAROSSA, Operation WERWOLF, Operation GREIF, and the escape organization known as ODESSA. He had also been involved in helping Skorzeny spirit Hitler's riches out of Germany and securing them from the rest of the world.

The invasion of Russia in 1941 proved to be Hitler's Waterloo. By the late winter of 1944, the war seemed lost.

Between the thirteenth and fifteenth of February 1945, during the Allied firebombing of Dresden, all three of the Lugoff children were killed. They were incinerated.

During the Battle of Berlin in April 1945, SS-Obersturmführer Lugoff had been one of the three million German soldiers captured by the Russians. He had been used in forced labor reconstruction for years in Stalingrad, and then was released in 1950 into what was then known as East Germany.

But his troubles did not end with his release from captivity.

The East German Staatssicherheit shortly picked him up. The Staatssicherheit were commonly referred to as *the Stasi.*

The Stasi, formally known as the Ministry for State Security, or Secret Police, was the official state security service of communist East Germany. A loyal arm of the Soviet Union, the Stasi forced Lugoff into recruitment by the most obscene of methods. The Stasi had imprisoned his wife, Ingrid, and with a combination of drugs and continual brutal rapes had forced her into prostitution. The Stasi promised to free Ingrid from their brothels, if only Wilhelm would become their willing intelligence asset.

Wilhelm complied and served the Stasi for eight years.

Pleased with his service and true to their word, the Stasi released Ingrid in 1958 from their brothel channels and back into Wilhelm's waiting arms.

Wolfram was born that year in East Berlin.

But the years had been extremely tough on his thirty-seven year old mother, and Ingrid died four years later from a combination of tuberculosis, hepatitis C, and low self-esteem.

No longer proud, but still defiant, former SS-Obersturmführer Wilhelm von Lugoff took little Wolfram and fled to Switzerland in 1962.

Securing employment as a salesman in an antiquarian shop, Wilhelm settled into a nondescript apartment in Geneva and raised his son as best he could.

Embarrassed by his escape, the Stasi hunted for their former agent for the next three years. During that time frame, a total of four Stasi assassins were sent to murder the former SS-Obersturmführer.

In Geneva, the first agent was found face down on the Rue de Berne with several stab wounds in his back.

Ten months later, a second agent was found beheaded and floating in the Rhone River.

Still another Stasi agent was found, a year later, with the back of his head blown off in a sedan parked outside the central post office on Rue du Mont-Blanc 18.

A fourth agent was found cut in half on the tracks of Geneva's Gare de Cornavin central railroad station.

Shortly after this last incident, the Stasi decided to just let the old Nazi alone.

When Wolfram turned eight years old, Wilhelm terminated his employment at the antiquarian shop and prioritized his life on solely providing a quality education for his son.

Wolfram was enrolled at the prestigious College du Leman university preparatory school in Versoix, Geneva. The College du Leman is a co-educational boarding school, where Wolfram excelled in mathematics, science, and sports.

The years flew by quickly, and Wolfram achieved placement in the top ten percent of his graduating class to be admitted to the University of Geneva.

At the end of four years, Wolfram graduated with a bachelor's degree in Applied Mathematics.

But for years he always wondered where his unemployed father found the funding to continue his education. He wondered why the monies seemed to always materialize.

One day Wolfram found out.

It was in 1979.

That year Wolfram turned of age.

He was now twenty-one, and legally considered an adult under Swiss law.

Former SS-Obersturmführer Wilhelm von Lugoff was sixty-one years old then, and had been diagnosed with pancreatic cancer. The cancer quickly achieved an aggressive nature, and Wilhelm was not expected to live but for a mere few months more.

On a Sunday in June, the dying Nazi brought his son into his study for a serious father-to-son talk.

"Wolfram," said Wilhelm.

"Yes father?"

"My son, I won't be around much longer to take care of you," explained Wilhelm.

Tears welled in Wolfram's eyes.

"Don't talk like that father. We will beat your cancer. The doctors will find a cure for you."

Wilhelm frowned.

"No son. I'm so very tired. It's my time. I've been waiting for the end to come. Only seeing you excel has been the greatest motivation to keep me living. But now you are doing fine. You are ready for the world. And it's time for me to be reunited with your mother."

"But father," Wolfram began.

"But nothing," Wilhelm said, cutting him off. "Listen to me now, son. There is something I need to pass on to you. There is something that will take care of you throughout your life. It is your inheritance, son. It is your birthright."

Wolfram was intrigued.

"What is it, father?"

Wilhelm sat down at his desk and opened the center drawer. Inside he retrieved a small white envelope and handed it to his son.

"But what is this, father?"

Looking at the envelope, Wilhelm said, "Open it, my son."

Wolfram slit the envelope open with his thumbnail, and peered into it.

Inside the envelope was a key.

He turned the envelope over and allowed the key to drop out into his hand.

It was a bank safety deposit box key.

"What is this, father?" asked Wolfram.

The old Nazi looked lovingly at his son.

"That key is to a safety deposit box located in the Swiss National Bank on Rue de la Croix d'Or 19," explained his father.

Wolfram studied the key.

"Well, what's in the box, father?" asked Wolfram.

"My son, inside that box you will find three separate files."

"The first file is a ledger of bank correspondence."

"The second file is of transaction receipts."

"The last file is of account numbers for the funds secured to three branch offices of the Swiss National Bank. One is in Zurich, one in Basel, and this one in Geneva."

"Each account has a separate number."

"All funds from these accounts have been transferred by me into your name as the sole beneficiary. A lot of the funds are still in gold."

Wolfram looked bewildered.

"Gold?" asked Wolfram.

"Yes, gold. Bars of gold," explained his father.

"All the bank certificates are in your name, assigning all the accounts to you. The account numbers are there in the safety deposit box, along with signatory authority provided by me to you. This allows you, as the sole owner of the box, unbridled access to all the accounts. And now, you have the key."

Wolfram asked, "Well, how much is it, father?"

The old Nazi thought for a moment.

"Son, I really don't know. These funds were entrusted to me at the end of the war by my commander. In 1944, they were valued at twenty-eight million American dollars."

Wolfram stared at his father.

"Today, I really don't know how much it's worth. I have used the money for us to live on all these years, and for your education."

Wolfram said, "Father, what will I do with all that money?"

Former SS-Obersturmführer Wilhelm von Lugoff looked seriously at his son, and explained.

"Live your life to the fullest, my son. Meet a wonderful young lady and fall in love. Get married. Raise a family. Give them all the best education money can buy. Make your life happy, my son."

The old Nazi was getting emotional now.

"Make your mother and me proud. And if you can, tell your children who we were, and what we fought for. Tell them about our cause. Tell them how much we sacrificed for our Fatherland. Tell them…about their birthright."

"Whatever you do son, stay away from the Russian communists."

"They are treachery at its worst."

"They destroyed our beloved Fatherland."

"They destroyed me."

"They destroyed your sainted mother."

"The communists are never to be trusted."

Wolfram closed his fist around the key, and stared into his father's strikingly clear jade green eyes.

"If I can father, I will avenge you and mother. I will make them pay."

The old Nazi pondered for a moment.

"There are some other items in the safety deposit box that you need to know about as well."

Wolfram asked, "What are they, father?"

"There's a sheet of instructions and a key, my son. The key is for a storage garage on the Rue Bergalonne, near the Patek Philippe Museum. I have prepaid the rent on that unit for the next ten years."

"Well, what's in the garage, father?"

The old Nazi's face became deadly serious.

"Inside the storage unit are some of my old belongings, uniforms and such, and also a machine. Under a large tarpaulin in the back, is a very special device. It's about the size of a small automobile. It looks sort of like a very large bell. Its military operational term was Die Glocke."

"What?" asked Wolfram.

Wilhelm said, "I was entrusted by my commander to safeguard Die Glocke. It is a machine that was created to stabilize fissionable materials for the Third Reich."

"Oh," said Wolfram.

The old man scratched his head and looked at his son, not sure if he should go on.

"That was the official story anyway. But, I was told that through operational testing, another use for Die Glocke was discovered."

"What would that be, father?" asked Wolfram.

The dying man said, "I was told, that Die Glocke could actually open a portal through time itself."

"What?" Wolfram asked incredulously.

"Yes son, it is true. I was told that Die Glocke was a type of transporter to the past or to the future. Through testing, Die Glocke was found to be able to propel a man into the fourth dimension. It is a sort of *time machine* if you will."

"We believed that there could be enormous military operational implications for Die Glocke. We planned to transport select troops into the past in order to conduct precise special operations. We felt these select missions could guarantee total victory and win the war for the Fatherland."

"The engineer in charge of the V-2 missiles and Die Glocke was General Hans Kammler. It is even believed that his disappearance at the end of the war had something to do with this. Some said he transported himself to the future, and then sent the machine back to the present."

"Of course, I found all that hard to believe. But a lot of research went into the construction, and I tell you this only as a historical fact. Perhaps one day you will bequeath Die Glocke to a museum, or to a scientific institute for further research."

Wolfram couldn't believe what he was hearing.

“Whatever you do my son, do not ever let Die Glocke fall into the hands of the Russians. If what my commander said was true, Die Glocke — in the proper hands — could change the destiny of the world forever.”

Wolfram was startled. He had never known of his father to exaggerate before. Everything his father had ever told him had always turned out to be true. He had no reason to doubt his father’s word on anything.

Yet this was truly amazing!

Whatever this Die Glocke was, he vowed that he would hold onto its secrets, and discover its mysteries.

So here he was, thirty-four years later, a retired career Foreign Service Officer and former United States Ambassador to Malaysia, now serving as a professor at the University of Zurich.

Wolfram von Lugoff, operating under the cover alias of Simon Watlington, was actually enjoying teaching the upper-level class on international terrorism.

His father would be so proud.

CHAPTER FOUR

CAIRO INTERLUDE

Egypt is considered a major non-NATO ally of the United States government. The US currently gives a foreign aid package to Egypt of approximately $1.5 billion. The majority of this aid is in money, and is supposed to be used for providing "peace and security" and "combating terrorism." Military assistance is also part of the aid package provided to Egypt from the United States. The Egyptian bureaucrats who decide how to use these funds occupy the seat of government in the capital city of Cairo. The Egyptian Arabic meaning of the name *Cairo* is *the Vanquisher.*

Anyone who is familiar with the Bible knows of Egypt's storied past and its place in history. It is a fantastic tourist destination, and Cairo is the gateway. Cairo is not only famous for the pyramids of Giza and the great sphinx, but also for opera, theater, film, museums, nightclubs, and sports — with football being the most popular. It currently is the largest city in the entire Arab world, with the Nile River flowing right through it.

The Nile is a popular tourist site, not only for its history, but for its famous floating restaurants. Customers can make their reservations for dinner, and also get a custom cruise on the Nile. One of the most popular of these establishments is Pharaohs.

Pharaohs is a barge type floating restaurant located right next to TGI Fridays and the Grand Café. This elegant platform sets sail from its dock every night and proceeds down the legendary River Nile. It sails around until the meal and the evening are done, and then returns to its dock. The restaurant serves a delicious buffet in the a-la-carte style. The entertainment revue includes singers, whirling dervishes, and belly dancers.

First introduced in the thirteenth century during the Ottoman Empire, whirling dervishes are men with elaborately decorated smocks, who spin around and twirl the ends of their garments outward in remembrance of God, as a type of movement meditation. The practice started as a mystical Islamic religious order, but soon morphed into many theatrical troupes for the tourist trade. The whirling dervishes resemble grandiose spinning tops.

James Ross was sitting at the bar of Pharaohs waiting for dinner to begin. He was dressed in a black suit coat and black trousers. His white cotton shirt had tiny blue pinstripes running vertically, and the collar was cinched with a narrow black necktie. He had removed his black leather shoes at the restaurant entrance, as had everyone else.

Ross heard the music start and twisted around on his stool to face the dance floor. He didn't know much about whirling dervishes, but he did know a thing or two about belly dancers.

The dancer's name was Emuishere. She was a very athletic twenty-three year old Egyptian woman. Emuishere was five feet two inches tall, with a gorgeous figure. Her entire body exuded health, energy, and vitality. She had very long shiny black tresses which reached to the middle of her exquisitely sensuous back. Her face was beautiful—crested with thin wisps of painted brows that sat atop two radiant eyes framed by long lashes. Her smile was to die for.

Emuishere was robed in a very revealing red Egyptian Bedleh costume. The Bedleh consisted of a bra, belt, and skirt. Emuishere's elastic belt was sewn into the skirt at the hips. Attached around her Dionysian waist was a thin gold chain with tiny silver coins. The coins jingled at every hip gyration.

The skirt was flimsy, sheer, and split at both sides down to the ankles. At times her sweat caused the fabric to cling to her amply developed bare buttocks and thighs.

She was dancing barefoot, and displayed a gold bracelet around her left ankle, and two gold rings on the toes of her right foot.

She sported a pair of Sagat finger cymbals on each hand which *"ching-chinged"* to the beat of the music.

Her bra was tiny and tight, making her bosom all the more pronounced and voluptuous. You couldn't help but notice the outline of her erect nipples.

Emuishere was writhing to a popular Awwady musical number. The music started to increase in tempo as Emuishere enticingly swirled and gyrated into a position directly in front of Ross.

Ross watched as Emuishere shimmied and shivered in front of him. Her abdominal muscles were pulsating and grinding as the rhythmic beat grew faster and faster. She crossed her arms in front of her face and wildly flipped her long hair, showering Ross with rivulets of her sweat. Ross tried to focus on her navel, but was having a hard time concentrating.

Emuishere was smiling as she *"ching-chinged"* her finger cymbals at him. The tempo increased to a feverish pitch, and Emuishere elegantly swung around and arched over backwards at the hips. She twirled her arms and hands in front of Ross in a rhythmic sexual pulse. Her breasts were swathed in sweat now, and straining at the tiny bra. Small droplets of Emuishere's sweat were being flicked off into Ross's stoic face.

Ross smiled and maintained his composure. A single drop of sweat originated at his right eyebrow and trickled down to his neck.

Then the tempo abruptly changed, and Emuishere righted herself up and twirled frolicsomely away, *"ching-chinging"* to the offstage exit.

Ross smiled and stood up, clapping his hands after her, along with the thirty other dinner guests.

US Army Special Forces Captain James Ross had been in Cairo for the past three weeks. He was on a clandestine mission to gather intelligence on the whereabouts of suspected al-Qaeda assassin Fazul Musa al-Adel. Al-Adel was wanted by the United States government for the murder of three American soldiers at a café in Abbottabad, Pakistan.

Announcements were made by the master of ceremonies, and then the patrons were bidden to the dinner tables. Ross was escorted to one of the smaller corner tables.

Waiters were already at the tables, laying out various trays of appetizers and drinks.

"Can I get anything else for you, sir?" asked the waiter in passing.

Ross had asked the next question at dozens of restaurants throughout Southeast and Southwest Asia. He enjoyed the routine and loved the responses. Mostly though, he loved the soup.

"Do you have French onion soup tonight?" inquired Ross.

The waiter looked at Ross and smiled.

"Why, yes sir. The best French onion soup in all of Cairo," said the waiter proudly.

"Okay. I'll have the French onion soup, with a large thin slice of cheese melted over the top," said Ross, returning the waiter's smile.

The waiter looked at Ross as two other couples joined him at the table.

"What did I just hear — French onion soup? You have French onion soup? That sounds really good. Bring us each one too," said the male companion of one of the couples.

The waiter smiled.

"Wait a minute sir," said the man from the other couple. "Bring my wife and me a bowl of that also, but hold the cheese please. We're watching our cholesterol."

The waiter smiled and bowed. He hurried off to the kitchen with the soup requests.

The two couples took their seats on either side of Ross. They were American, middle-aged tourists, and quickly set about introducing themselves around the table and engaging in small talk.

Ross joined in the conversation.

Soon another patron joined their table and sat directly opposite of Ross.

He was a lone male in his late twenties.

Standing at five feet eleven inches tall and weighing one hundred and seventy pounds, the young man was of Saudi Arabian nationality. He was wearing a slightly baggy light blue suit, with an open collared white silk shirt. He had a dark, swarthy complexion, with closely cropped, greasy black hair. His ears stuck awkwardly out from the sides of his head. He looked as if he hadn't shaved for three weeks. His whiskers masked the pockmark effects of being unvaccinated for smallpox in childhood.

The young man did not engage in the banality of the conversations, but instead focused an intensively arrogant stare at Ross.

This was no tourist.

It was Fazul Musa al-Adel, the al-Qaeda assassin.

The other two couples continued talking and sharing information about where they were from, and how much they were enjoying their vacations.

Ross ceased talking and stared back at al-Adel.

Suddenly an alternate conversation started to take place at the table.

"So, American, you are looking for me, yes?" asked al-Adel with a heavy accent.

"I am," coldly replied Ross. "You're wanted for murder."

"Really? And what are the United States and your President going to do about it? Are you going to arrest me?" inquired al-Adel in a mocking tone.

The other two couples continued with their small talk, being completely oblivious to the fervent discussion between Ross and al-Adel. Ross placed both of his hands completely flat on the table next to his silverware.

"I don't think it will come to that, Fazul," seethed Ross.

Al-Adel snickered.

"Let me tell you something, American cowboy. I am going to kill you here and cut your head off in the kitchen. Then I am going to post the photos for all the world to see."

Ross cocked an eyebrow.

"Really? So says the seducer of young boys."

Al-Adel's face flushed crimson.

"What do you mean?"

Ross replied, "Not only are you a murderer, but you're also a pervert and rapist, Fuzzy. You get your kicks by torturing little boys."

Al-Adel was enraged now, and started to rise up out of his seat.

Just then the waiter appeared with five bowls of steaming hot French onion soup.

Pointing to the couple on his right side, Ross said, "Okay, I think you guys didn't want the cheese, right sir?"

“That’s right young man. We’re watching our diet. But I damn well wish I could have some of that there cheese because it sure smells good!”

The waiter finished by placing a bowl of onion soup in front of Ross, and then quickly left for the kitchen.

Al-Adel leaned forward in his chair.

“I tell you American, you will not live to see the dawn.”

“Well,” smiled Ross, “I’d better enjoy my soup then.”

With his right hand, Ross picked up his soup spoon and dipped it in the bowl of onion soup.

Al-Adel became infuriated. He reached across the table and knocked Ross’s bowl of French onion soup to the floor.

“Allahu Akbar!” screamed al-Adel rising out of his chair while pulling a Tokarev pistol from underneath his suit coat.

Ross sprang to his feet like a panther.

With his left hand, he picked up the crystal plate that his soup bowl had rested on, and smashed it in half on the forehead of the terrorist. The plate shattered, and left Ross with a jagged end in his left hand.

He still had a hold of the soup spoon in his right.

With a huge sweep, Ross brought his left arm crossways and slashed the serrated edge of the broken plate across al-Adel’s throat.

Blood sprayed across the table.

Al-Adel’s hands flew up to his throat as his pistol automatically dropped and clattered across the floor

Simultaneously, Ross thrust out with the spoon in his right hand, gouging it into al-Adel’s left eye.

Al-Adel screamed in agony as Ross surged across the table and followed him to the floor.

Ross continued shoving the stainless steel soup spoon into al-Adel's left eye socket.

Now on top of the man, Ross hooked his left thumb into al-Adel's right eye socket and squashed the eyeball like someone would squash a grape.

Ross pressed and shoved, turning al-Adel's eye sockets into squishy, gooey, inkwells of slime.

Completely blinded, al-Adel fainted as Ross put both of his hands on the broken plate and grated the serrated edge back and forth across al-Adel's throat — again and again — gruesomely severing the man's jugular vein.

Blood flowed freely, and soon the floor was awash in the wet, sticky, metallic-smelling, vermilion gore.

Ross got up from the floor.

"Sorry I ruined your evening," apologized Ross to the clearly shocked table guests.

Before anyone could fathom what had just unfolded, Ross walked quietly to the rear exit and climbed over the port side railing. He pushed himself out and splashed feet first into the warm waters of the welcoming River Nile.

Pharaohs floating restaurant was a good hundred yards from shore. Ross judged the distance and began the crawl stroke.

Soon Ross was climbing up on one of the dock ladders. He quickly walked down the aged, creaking gang planks of the unknown pier.

Upon reaching the end of the pier, Ross held his arm over his head and hailed a taxi.

He glanced at his beloved Benrus watch on his left wrist.

Its luminous blade hands alerted him that it was ten-thirty in the evening.

As the taxi pulled up, Ross had only one instruction for the driver.

"Take me somewhere that serves great French onion soup."

CHAPTER FIVE

USAOG

Close to Odenton Maryland, and right next to Highway 175, is the United States military installation known as Fort Meade. It is named after General George G. Meade, who commanded the Union Army of the Potomac during the American Civil War. General Meade is perhaps best known as the commander who defeated Confederate General Robert E. Lee during the infamous Battle of Gettysburg in 1863.

Fort Meade is a rather typical military installation — as far as military installations go.

You will find the usual military facilities located there: barracks, hospital, clinics, motor pools, gymnasiums, post exchanges, libraries, firing ranges, and of course various military units.

Some of these military units include the Defense Information Systems Agency, the 70th Intelligence Wing Headquarters, the Cyber

Command, the 902d Military Intelligence Group, the Central Clearance Facility, and the Defense Courier Service.

There's a dirt jogging trail in the woods that runs around the golf course and encircles the installation. When you run on the trail, you must be careful not to step on the turtles that always seem to materialize after a hard rain. Halfway around the trail, you can take a left through the woods and run straight into Jim's Hideaway restaurant. Jim's Hideaway is famous for its daily special of all the crab you can eat for $32.00. Further on, you can take a detour and run straight into the cryptographic intelligence agency known as the National Security Agency.

Fort George G. Meade is the preeminent military intelligence installation in the United States today.

Across from the movie theater and next to the parade field is a very long, multi-storied, red brick building, shaped like a giant inverted "L" letter. This building is the home for the 902d Military Intelligence Group and the Central Clearance Facility. It is also home for the USAOG.

USAOG, otherwise known as the United States Army Operational Group, or Ops Group, is the premier HUMINT organization in the Department of Defense today.

HUMINT, or Human Intelligence, deals with information provided and collected by human sources.

USAOG members conduct missions in human intelligence, signals intelligence, geospatial intelligence, science and technology intelligence, cyber intelligence, counterintelligence, and just about every other intelligence discipline there is. They were even known at times to have a remote viewing unit.

Special Forces Captain James Ross kept his aged automobile keys securely fastened to his US Army issued identification tag chain around his neck.

Carefully, he pulled the chain up and over his head.

Meticulously guiding the key into the lock, he turned it clockwise until the silver door knob rose shakily with an audible popping sound.

Ross opened the left side drivers' door and squished down on the cold vinyl of the frayed ivy gold colored bucket seats.

Leaning forward, he slid the ignition key in and turned it to the right until the engine sputtered to life.

With his left hand, he released the hand parking brake under the dashboard by pulling it out slightly, and turning it down and to the left, while letting it glide forward.

Boldly he pressed twice on the throttle with his right foot, giving the car some gasoline, before carefully depressing the black release button on the floor automatic shifter and engaging it into reverse.

Ross backed out ever so carefully to avoid scratching the Mercedes and Jaguars that always seemed to park ever so close to him.

He pressed the black release button once again, and shifted into drive.

Cautiously he steered the car through his apartment parking lot maze and out into traffic.

Ross's pride and joy was his car: a vintage 1968 Ford Mustang fastback, still touting its original, but faded, lime gold paint.

He was taking the car through its paces now, driving hard and fast towards Fort Meade. The Mustang was handling well, with the luminescent needle unwaveringly fluttering at sixty miles an hour behind the scratched face of the plastic speedometer gauge.

The forty-five year old Ford was barely showing its age as Ross held the steering wheel steady and pushed the small six cylinder engine onward.

Ross recently had the punctured muffler repaired, but the engine still emitted a booming throaty sound that gave the car a hot rod type affect.

The antique car had long ago lost its immunity to road noise, and just about every drive made Ross's ears feel as if he were experiencing the roars at the Indianapolis Motor Speedway.

He twisted the steel knob on the archaic AM radio, trying to find a static-free station. A Coldplay song came on, and Ross finally settled back to enjoy the ride.

Ross was always cautious.

He realized his old Ford could develop a multitude of mechanical problems at any time, leaving him stranded on the road.

Ross thought that deep down inside…psychologically…he was in love with that thrill.

I must be crazy, he thought.

Most officers he knew drove BMW's or Audi's. But he loved his old Mustang, and could never imagine himself driving anything else.

Ross's thoughts drifted off to his last mission.

It had been in Cairo.

A man was killed.

The man was a terrorist.

He was an assassin in al-Qaeda.

His name was Fazul Musa al-Adel.

Ross did not consider himself a warrior.

He never wanted to kill anyone.

He did not enjoy it.

He did not look forward to it.

Ross looked at himself differently.

I'm just a simple soldier, he thought.

But this last mission had become wretched.

The killing was hand-to-hand.

It was brutal and macabre.

I killed the man like an animal.

Worse than an animal, he thought.

But Ross could not allow himself to be troubled by the killing.

It was war, he thought.

Terrible things happen every day in war.

Some of Ross's friends had endured incredible traumas during the wars. A few were suffering with Post Traumatic Stress Disorder.

Ross knew that PTSD was serious and nothing to fool around with.

He was respectful of it.

But, he also knew that if he ever revealed anything like that, he would be signing his own exit visa from the Special Forces community.

It didn't matter what he was *feeling.*

How could you lead soldiers in combat if you admitted to having PTSD?

SF troopers expected their commanders to be fearless.

There was no room to coddle someone in the teams.

SF was not an encounter group.

Everyone had to pull their own weight.

If you couldn't hack it anymore in the field, maybe SF branch would take pity on you and assign you to the Pentagon.

There, you could walk around with your coffee cup attached to your index finger and pretend to be important. You could use up time until retirement.

Ross realized he was oversimplifying the situation, and covering it up by making light of it. He had no animosity towards headquarters staff personnel. He just knew what he wanted, and that was to be in the field.

But all boys have to grow up someday.

Ross had unofficially been seeing a psychiatrist whom he had met while working out at the post gym.

He had been receiving counseling, but swore the physician to secrecy for fear of jeopardizing his job.

The psychiatrist explained to him that would never happen. He said the Army understood and wanted to treat psychological problems in its soldiers nowadays.

But Ross still kept it quiet.

He wished his girlfriend, Lin Sparrow, was there to talk to.

Man, I miss Lin.

She's the one person I can talk to about this stuff.

Lin doesn't judge.

Lin listens to me.

Lin makes me feel good.

She just understands me.

Ross had worked too hard to get to where he was to throw it all away now.

I want to hang around for at least twenty or so years, he thought.

I can't even imagine any other job except being a special operations soldier.

I just have to will the stress away with my mind.

The old Green Beret mind discipline training again, he smiled.

Everybody talks about PTSD these days.

You would think that every soldier has it from watching the news shows.

Well, if I have it, I don't give a damn.

Someone has to do this job.

Someone has to serve.

If not me, then who will?

Ross was rapidly approaching the front gate of Fort George G. Meade United States Army Installation.

He saw the front gate "Reduced Speed Limit" sign, and slowed down to ten miles per hour.

As Ross drove up and over the speed bump, he leaned forward reaching into his back pocket and pulled out his Velcro olive drab wallet.

The black uniformed Department of Defense contract security guard at the front gate looked at Ross as he struggled to manually roll down the passenger side window.

Ross held out his plastic laminated US Army identification card for the security guard.

The security guard took the card and held it in his hand. He ran an electronic hand-held scanner over its face.

Beep!

"All right, thank you Captain," said the security guard, returning his card and waving him forward.

Ross stuck his ID card back inside his wallet and rolled up his window. He carefully drove through the security gate area.

Soon Ross was motoring behind the huge USAOG building and into the rear parking lot.

He found a vacant spot and pulled in, turning off the engine.

Getting out of the fastback, Ross looked at his wristwatch.

Ross's timepiece was a new Swiss Benrus Type I Class A diving model that Lin Sparrow had given him. Lin had the watch outfitted with a custom stainless steel Olongapo bracelet, engraved with his name and SF team number.

It was ten minutes before nine o'clock in the morning.

The commander Ross worked for allowed all his soldiers to exercise every morning from zero-six-thirty to zero-seven-thirty hours; he allowed forty-five minutes to conduct personal hygiene, and forty-five minutes to sit down and eat breakfast. The daily morning staff meeting started at ten o'clock, and lasted no more than an hour.

Snow was floating down slowly and playfully over the National Capital Region. The temperature was a freezing twenty-nine degrees Fahrenheit.

Ross was wearing the uniform-of-the-day: his blue Army Class A's under a long black Army issued trench coat.

Ross had graduated from Texas Christian University of Fort Worth eight years ago, majoring in political science. This led to his original commissioning in Army Intelligence. He branch transferred to Special Forces as soon as he could.

His American father had been old-school Special Forces, and his mother was from Thailand. Both of his parents had passed away long ago. He inherited from them his piercing dark brown eyes, brown hair that would never stay put, and a knack for picking up languages. He had always been proud of being half Thai and half American, half East and half West.

Ross shoved his hands into his trench coat pockets and hunched up his shoulders against the bitter cold.

Walking purposefully, he quickly crossed the parking lot and entered the USAOG building.

He bounded up the three flights of stairs and walked down the hall to the left, stopping in front of the huge steel door that controlled access to the USAOG offices.

The offices of USAOG were contained inside a Sensitive Compartmented Information Facility, commonly referred to as a SCIF. SCIF's are secure areas with access controls established because classified information is routinely handled and discussed everywhere inside.

Ross lifted the hinged plastic cover off of the cipher lock on the door and punched in his secure access numbers. The cipher lock engaged, and with a tug on the handle the door opened. He allowed the door to close behind him with a metallic *"click"* and walked into the main lobby.

Ross walked down the hall and entered the men's room, checking himself out in the mirror. He looked at the shards of hair hanging in front of his eyes and frowned. Franticly, he ran his fingers through his thick shock of hair and tried to push the dark brown bangs back off his forehead.

After two seconds they just fell back down in more disarray.

Oh the hell with it, he thought.

Ross's office was a nondescript affair. It was quietly nestled next to the USAOG Deputy Commander's office, and across the hall from the Director of Collection Operations.

Because of his intelligence and special operations background, Ross found a home in the Operations Support Branch. His job was to conduct special activities as required to combat terrorism. The terminology *special activities* meant that he could engage in not only overt and clandestine means, but also covert means for mission accomplishment.

That was fancy talk to say he was a soldier who could go undercover if need be to fight the bad guys.

He would even receive an Officer Evaluation Report with a secret classification out of it, which should enhance his career considerably.

Secrets, he thought.

Ross wondered about the secret world he had chosen for himself.

Secrets.

The idea was that somehow secrets made us safer.

Didn't just being stronger than your enemies make you safer?

But that wasn't allowed anymore today, at least in theory.

The United States was downsizing the military again, while at the same time freely supplying advanced fighter jets to Egypt, a country which preaches the total destruction of Israel. Not to mention the billions of dollars in aid the United States continues to give to countries like Pakistan, who harbored our deadliest enemy for the past twenty years — Osama bin Laden.

Could secrets keep us safer?

Sure.

But they were completely useless if the people in the field didn't get the information in a timely manner to make a difference to save lives.

You have to keep things in perspective.

How could all the compartmented secrets in the world stop a mob of radical Muslim extremists from overrunning the US Embassy in Benghazi?

Critical thinking and reality testing usually worked better, along with a company or two from the 82d Airborne Division.

Government agencies are known for stove piping intelligence at the top. After all, knowledge is power. All that did was deny critical information to the trigger pullers at the bottom.

Government bureaucrats sometimes saved their careers by excessively hiding their incompetency behind secret labels.

Secrets.

Ross sat down in the large black imitation leather upholstered swivel chair behind his oak desk, and powered up his official US government computer.

The Dell Computer Company had won the contract several years ago, and was the computer of choice for the US Departments of Defense and State. The Information Management folks at the Defense Department had long ago established secure mainframe communications support throughout all US military installations worldwide.

Ross inserted his identification card into the common access card or CAC reader, and securely logged on.

He scrolled through his email message traffic, answering those messages that he could quickly, and saving those that required more personal attention.

Next, Ross reached for his black plastic STU III key and inserted it into the secure telephone unit third generation on his desk. He turned the key clockwise establishing a secure electronic mode. Finally, he picked up the receiver and punched in the code numbers to check his secure messages.

Ross listened intently.

He had only one telephonic message. It was from the executive officer informing him that the daily staff meeting was cancelled, and that he was to meet the commander in his office today at zero-nine-thirty hours. The meeting was to discuss Operation TIMELESS TERROR.

TIMELESS TERROR was the codename given for the secret operation involving a terrorist financier. The war in Afghanistan was being fought as a full-blown counterinsurgency mission. The operations involved combating certain hybrid threats such as cross-border terrorists, criminal elements, and proprietary money laundering.

Operation TIMELESS TERROR was surmised to involve all of these hybrid threats.

Ross looked at his Benrus wristwatch. Its luminous blade hands reminded him that it was twenty minutes past nine o'clock.

Guess I'd better get moving, thought Ross.

Ross turned the STU III key counterclockwise and pulled it out of the phone. He pocketed the key and logged off of his Dell computer, securing his CAC card.

He looked around his office for a second, making sure he had not left any classified material unsecure. When he was satisfied, Ross got up and left his office, locking the door behind him.

Ross turned left and walked down the carpeted corridor towards the USAOG commander's office.

The commander did not have a secretary. Rather, he utilized his executive officer, Major Breck Walker, to control access to his office. The door to Major Walker's office always seemed to be open. Today was no exception.

Ross stopped inside the executive officer's doorway and waved a hand.

"Good morning Major Walker," said Ross.

Major Walker looked up from his stack of intelligence summaries, orders, evaluations, and SPECAT special category priority messages and smiled.

"Good morning Jim. Here for your conference with the boss, huh?" said Major Walker.

"Yep, I'm getting ready to go in now."

Ross paused a second, leaning against the door frame and asked, "Is there anything special I should know about this?"

Major Walker leaned back in his rattan swivel chair. He mechanically picked up his USAA labeled ceramic cup full of steaming Pakistani coffee and took a long, slow sip. He smacked his lips, and then placed the cup back down onto a souvenir bamboo coaster from Mali.

"Well," said Major Walker contemplating, "I hope you like cuckoo clocks and chocolates."

Ross straightened up and furrowed his brow in concentration.

"Okay sir. Thanks," said Ross, "I think."

Ross smiled and walked to the commander's door.

He paused in front of the dark mahogany door and squared his shoulders back.

Ross looked at his Benrus. Its luminous hands announced to him that it was nine-twenty-nine.

He reached forward with his right hand and knocked three times.

"Come on in," yelled the commander.

Ross turned the door knob and entered the commander's office, closing the door behind him.

The commander's office sported a plush wall-to-wall woodland brown tufted carpet with the seal of the Department of the Army woven into the center of it.

Modern brass floor lamps in each of the four corners cast a warm, trusting glow about the room.

The walls were wood paneled in rustic oak.

The far left wall was festooned with years of military unit plaques and memorabilia of the commander's past successes in the army. Side by side were framed certificates indicating Colonel Winbolt's membership in both the Military Intelligence and the Special Forces Regiments. On the right wall were hung his numerous graduation certificates from his military schools and colleges.

The back wall was framed by four massive bay windows that overlooked the parade field across the street.

In front of the bay windows was the commander's enormous oak desk. To the right of the desk was positioned the United States flag and the Military Intelligence Corps flag complete with regimental streamers.

Behind the desk was sitting Colonel Winbolt in a tall-backed oak chair with caster wheels on its legs. The chair was upholstered in dark brown leather with brass rivets running up and down its sides.

In front of the desk were placed two similar looking chairs, but smaller in stature. Behind these, in the center of the room, sat a large dark-green-dyed leather upholstered sofa. In front of the sofa sat an oblong oak coffee table.

Ross spotted the chairs in front of the commander's desk and stopped just to the right of one at the position of attention.

He snapped his right hand up in a crisp salute.

"Captain Ross reporting, sir," said Ross respectfully.

The commander looked up at Ross and returned the salute.

"Sit. Sit down," said Colonel Winbolt motioning with his gnarled hands.

Colonel Henry Alfred Winbolt was fifty years old. He was six feet tall with a painfully thin frame. His close cut hair was snow white and thinning on the crown. His sky blue eyes were inquisitive and probing, and aided by ever present reading glasses perched upon his hawk-like nose. His joints were continually on fire with crippling Reiter's Syndrome degenerative arthritis. Two years ago, he had to undergo bilateral knee replacements. Now he set off the security scanners at every civilian airport.

Winbolt also suffered from high blood pressure, high cholesterol, fractured vertebra, bulging discs, tinnitus, and sleep apnea. He tried his best to deny and hide all his maladies from the army doctors, as he feared a medical review board would force him into early retirement.

Constantly in pain, Colonel Winbolt self-medicated with weight lifting, martial arts, and Vicodin.

Winbolt was a career military intelligence officer with extensive special operations experience. He had been in the position of USAOG commander for the past year, having served at just about every echelon of command there was in the army. Winbolt was one of those gifted officers who was a War College graduate, had a master's degree in international studies from the Sorbonne, and was fluent in three languages. He had served ten years in special mission units, and was a former commander of the Intelligence Support Activity.

Winbolt was a man of few words. He had a reputation as a no-nonsense commander, who would step in front of a charging rhino to protect his soldiers.

"Good morning Jim. How are you today?" asked Colonel Winbolt.

Ross relaxed back in the chair.

“Doing well sir, thank you,” said Ross.

“Well, the reason you’re here is that we have information on an al-Qaeda paymaster operating in Switzerland.”

Colonel Winbolt studied his face for any response.

Ross’s expression remained like stone.

Winbolt leaned forward in his chair and shuffled through the folder in front of him. The folder had a red bordered Department of Defense cover sheet stapled on its front. The word “SECRET” was clearly printed in large red letters at the top and bottom. He pulled out two pages and studied them for a second.

“I take it you’re familiar with Operation TIMELESS TERROR?” asked Winbolt.

“Yes sir.”

Ross had been “read-on” to TIMELESS TERROR for a while.

“Good. Well, we have established connections from three branch offices of the Swiss National Bank to al-Qaeda financial section personnel operating out of Abbottabad, Pakistan. The Swiss branch offices are in Zurich, Basel, and Geneva.”

Winbolt shifted in his chair.

“It seems that funds, usually in gold bullion, find their way to agents operating through the Hawala banking system, which is basically a group of money brokers. They receive the gold and either trade for cash, or, in some cases actually pay their members in bullion. Bullion as you may know or not, is usually in the form of coins or bars. In this case, payments have always been made with gold bars.”

Winbolt took a breath.

"The list of payees reads like a who's who of Islamic militant groups. It includes Gulbuddin Hekmatyar, Quetta Shura Taliban, the Haqqani network, and Lashkar-e-Taiba. Last month, one of our assets was paid with one of the gold bars. He photographed it before he melted it down for disbursing."

Colonel Winbolt took off his reading glasses and placed them on his desk.

"The gold bar had the stampings of the Berlin Reichsbank on it. I'm talking about the 1943 Berlin Reichsbank. It was complete with Nazi eagle and Swastika."

Winbolt slid the photo of the gold bar across his desktop to Ross.

Ross leaned forward and picked up the photo. He could clearly make out the Nazi Reichsbank proof stampings on the precious metal.

Ross was mystified.

"We've confirmed this intelligence through other sources, namely interrogations of prisoners," said Winbolt.

"Disbursing funds to terrorists with gold...Nazi gold? This sounds like some kind of crazy movie plot," said Ross.

"It gets even better. We were able, through our considerable resources in banking circles, to actually pry loose from the Swiss the name of the account holder."

"Who is that?" asked Ross.

Winbolt put back on his reading glasses and searched through the folder. He pulled out a fragile piece of yellowed paper.

"You have to understand something," said Winbolt. "Getting information like this from the Swiss banking networks is like pulling hen's teeth."

Colonel Winbolt turned the paper over and continued scanning.

"It appears the owner of the accounts is a certain Mister Wolfram von Lugoff."

Ross asked, "Who is this Mister Lugoff?"

Winbolt put the aged paper down and looked at Ross from behind his reading glasses.

"We don't know," said Winbolt. "We can't find any records on him."

"None, sir?" asked Ross.

"None at all. It's as if Wolfram von Lugoff does not exist. But, research has found an SS-Obersturmführer Wilhelm von Lugoff from World War Two. He was a commando with Otto Skorzeny. He was awarded the Knight's Cross from the Russian Front. The list of his accolades goes on and on."

"Whatever happened to him?" asked Ross.

Winbolt peered at his dossier again.

"It looks like he was captured by the Russians at the end of the war. He was held in a Gulag prison for years, and then the trail goes cold. But if he were even alive today—he would be ninety-five years old."

"So, do we think this Wolfram Lugoff is related somehow to this World War Two Nazi officer?" asked Ross.

"It could be," said Winbolt, "but of course we have no proof. Through SIGINT, HUMINT, and now further confirmed with IMINT, we have ascertained that a major paymaster," Colonel Winbolt spread his hands wide, "and I mean *major paymaster,* is operating in Zurich, Switzerland. That's what we know for sure. What we think is that this man probably uses a nonofficial cover of being a college professor. But we haven't confirmed that piece of information yet. One source in particular says that the man actually is a college professor. But again, that information has not been completely confirmed."

Winbolt paused to look at the opened folder on his desk in front of him.

"I understand you were on a mission in Malaysia not too long ago, and have met Simon Watlington before?"

"Yes sir. He's the Ambassador to Malaysia," said Ross.

"Was," replied Winbolt squinting over his reading glasses.

"The Honorable Simon Watlington retired from the Foreign Service, and now just by coincidence holds a professor position at the University of Zurich."

"Just how well do you know Simon Watlington?" inquired Colonel Winbolt.

Ross's gaze shifted to somewhere behind Colonel Winbolt as he thought about that question for a moment.

Winbolt held up the palm of his hand as if to refocus Ross.

"Now don't get the wrong idea here, Jim. I'm not connecting Watlington to this al-Qaeda suspect. Okay? Watlington's record is impeccable. He's in the good-old-boy network from State. And he's clean as far as we're concerned. He has powerful friends in the current administration as well. He's retired from State now and teaching over there at the University of Zurich. And since you know him, he could be an ally in this for you."

Ross looked at Colonel Winbolt and replied, "Well sir, I was debriefed by him and his staff in Kuala Lumpur last summer, and I always thought he was a pretty competent individual."

Winbolt leaned back in his oak swivel chair and narrowed his gaze.

"That's what I mean. You guys are friends. Watlington can assist you in Zurich. It's in his blood. He's retired from thirty years in the Foreign Service. And he's got a lot of pull as a former ambassador. He's already been briefed about this situation and knows you're coming. He's signed on to provide any assistance he can."

Colonel Winbolt let that piece of information sink into Ross's mind for a few seconds. He was hoping any suspicions Ross may have had would jar loose to the surface.

"But the real questions are how is the gold from these accounts getting to the terrorists, and who in the hell is this Wolfram von Lugoff?" said Winbolt.

Colonel Winbolt stared straight into Ross's eyes.

"I want to smash this God damned terror payment pipeline. This gold finances al-Qaeda terrorists, and these al-Qaeda bastards are killing our people in Afghanistan and all over the world."

"Yes sir," said Ross.

"You're leaving tomorrow. I'm putting you on extended temporary duty in Switzerland. You'll be operating under the official cover of conducting a security survey for our consular agency in Zurich. I want you to send your situation reports daily on the SIPRNET."

Ross was well versed at using the Department of Defense Secure Internet Protocol Router Network for transmitting classified information.

"Your job is only to get the intelligence," said Winbolt.

"Yes sir."

"We need to prove who actually owns these accounts. And then, we can seize the assets under international law, since the monies are being used to finance terrorism. Once we do that, then INTERPOL will arrest the owner, or owners."

"INTERPOL, sir? The International Criminal Police Organization?" asked Ross.

"Yes. INTERPOL will make the initial arrest, and then hand whoever it is over to the FBI," said Winbolt. "Then they can be brought back to the US to stand trial as terrorist financiers."

"Yes sir," said Ross.

Colonel Winbolt leaned forward and placed his elbows on his desk. He folded his hands together in front of him.

"Major Walker has electronically sent this information securely and made a hardcopy of this folder for you. Pick it up from him on your way out."

"Any questions Jim?" asked Colonel Winbolt.

"No sir."

"Fine, that'll be all then," said Winbolt.

Ross immediately stood to the position of attention and saluted.

Colonel Winbolt smiled and returned the salute.

"Good luck son," said Winbolt.

Ross turned around and started to walk out.

"Oh Jim," said Winbolt.

Ross stopped and turned around.

"Be safe. And don't forget to use your friendship with Simon Watlington. He's a good source to have over there. He can possibly cut through any red tape and get things done quicker for you. He's a good ally to have."

"Yes sir," Ross replied.

Ross turned around and walked out of the commander's office, closing the door behind him.

Colonel Winbolt took off his reading glasses and tossed them onto his desktop. He swiveled his chair around and stared out of the windows to the parade field below.

He was troubled in his thoughts.

CHAPTER SIX

ENTER ZURICH

Ross's flight to Zurich departed right on time.

He flew out of New York's JFK International Airport on a United Airlines Airbus A330-300 as one of three hundred passengers. The highlight of the flight was the spectacular cuisine.

Ross was relaxing and leaning back in one of the luxurious business class seats when a gorgeous stewardess from down the aisle approached him.

This female flight attendant was wearing the international United Airlines uniform consisting of black high heeled shoes, dark blue nylons, dark blue knee-length skirt, dark blue jacket, and white open collar blouse. She topped the ensemble off with a small blue striped neck scarf and her golden flight wings, which were pinned above her left breast.

This particular air hostess was twenty-four years old and of Italian descent. She stood about five feet seven inches tall, and her weight was around one hundred and twenty-five pounds. Her hair was straight, shiny black, and shoulder length, with slanted bangs running across her forehead. She had dark brown eyes, a beautiful smile, and vibrantly white teeth. Her complexion was olive and healthy, and you could tell she was fit.

A plastic tag below her gold flight wings announced her name to be Sophia.

Ross remembered from his TCU college days that the name *Sophia* in the ancient Greek language meant *wisdom.*

"Would you care to order dinner from our menu, sir?" asked Sophia.

Ross inquired, "Umm, what are your specials today, Sophia?"

The stewardess smiled.

"We have a great tasting New York strip steak, and a sweet broiled mahi-mahi."

Ross thought for a moment.

"Okay Sophia, I'll have a medium New York strip, with a garden salad, please."

Sophia began to write down Ross's order on her small notepad.

"What kind of dressing would you like on your salad, sir?"

"Oh, how about some balsamic vinaigrette dressing?"

Sophia wrote Ross's request down.

"Very good sir, thank you. And to drink, sir?" asked Sophia.

"Let me have unsweetened iced tea, please," answered Ross.

Ross now asked the question he loved to ask at every restaurant he happened to find himself in. It was the same culinary cuisine question he has asked all across the world. He enjoyed the routine and loved the responses. Mostly though, he loved the soup.

"Do you have French onion soup today?" inquired Ross.

Sophia looked up from her notepad and smiled.

"Why yes, sir. The best French onion soup in all the friendly blue skies," she said proudly.

"Okay. I'll have the French onion soup, with a large thin slice of cheese melted over the top," said Ross returning her smile.

Sophia smiled back and said, "Yes sir. I'll have that right out for you."

After about twelve minutes the food arrived. Ross devoured every morsel of the absolutely delicious meal.

The flight was scheduled to take nine hours, putting Ross into Zurich at just before midnight local time.

He turned on his complimentary mini television and started watching Fox News.

Ross was just too wired to sleep.

Zurich is a marvelous city.

Founded by the Romans over two thousand years ago, Zurich has a population of almost two million, making it the largest city in Switzerland. It is one of the world's busiest financial centers, with its own stock exchange. Its low tax rate entices many overseas corporations to position headquarters there. The city is a smorgasbord of culture, boasting festivals, art galleries, museums, symphonies, theater, opera, ballet, and numerous sporting events.

Zurich is also the richest city in Europe, and the world's largest gold trading center.

The Zurich Airport is the most modern and largest international airport in all of Switzerland, with outstanding customer service.

Ross breezed through Swiss customs with his black diplomatic passport. He was traveling under an official cover, and Swiss customs was good at extending all courtesies to traveling diplomats.

He already had his luggage, since he always traveled light with an overhead carry-on bag, and usually managed to squeeze everything he needed into it.

Exchange rate signs were posted on several walls. In Switzerland, American dollars were accepted everywhere. Currently, one Swiss Franc was the equivalent of about one dollar and six cents US

Ross walked towards the nearest airport exit, but stopped short to look at the temperature gauge on the huge green and gold overhead Rolex wall clock.

The monitor showed the temperature outside to be a cool twenty-nine degrees Fahrenheit.

The double glass doors of the nearest airport exit hissed open and a gust of frigid wintry air hit Ross and made him catch his breath.

Ross surveyed the outdoor scene.

Large flakes of snow were floating down and circling with a blustery wind swishing back and forth in front of the airport terminal.

Drivers with their Mercedes-Benz taxis were everywhere, calmly waiting inside their rides for fares.

This is strange, thought Ross.

There is no feeding frenzy?

This was Ross's first trip to Switzerland, and the subdued taxi atmosphere was unlike almost everywhere else Ross had been in the world. In Southeast and Southwest Asia, taxi drivers would push, shove, and cram in front of him, offering their best fares for anywhere.

Interestingly, a tenacious driver caught Ross's attention by waving a red cowboy-styled handkerchief-bandana out of the window of his Mercedes-Benz sedan. It looked like the same style handkerchief Ross always carried himself.

The man quickly got out of his car and shuffled over to Ross. He was wearing a large gray parka with his head completely covered by the furry snorkel hood. As he got closer, the man pulled off the hood revealing his features.

The man was young, and appeared to be in his early thirties, perhaps thirty-three. He had a medium frame, and stood at around five feet ten inches tall. His smooth dark skin immediately reminded Ross of a full blooded Filipino. His black hair was clean and neatly groomed, shoulder length, and parted in the middle. The man looked as if he hadn't shaved in a week or two. He smiled easily and displayed pearly white teeth. His face had a strange glow about it that immediately put Ross at ease. His eyes were dark brown and reassuringly gently. He was wearing what looked like an old surplus United States Air Force issued parka, faded blue jeans, and black rubber snow boots that buckled in the front.

"Hello Captain Ross," said the smiling taxi driver.

I must be dreaming, thought Ross.

The taxi driver thumped his chest with his thumb.

"It's me, sir," said the driver.

It was Emanuel.

Emanuel Mesiyas was the taxi driver who Ross had met on his last mission to the Philippines. He had flown Ross through a severe typhoon, and stood side by side with him through a bloody firefight with Abu Sayyaf terrorists.

Emanuel thrust out his right hand and Ross cheerfully shook it.

"Emanuel, my God! What in the world are you doing here?"

Emanuel smiled and said, "Well sir, it's an interesting story all right. You see, my cousin, Lailani, had this restaurant in Manila called Best Eats. Anyway, she was having some really bad money problems, but then she met a Swiss businessman. Well, one thing led to another, and they started dating, and then got married. Not too long after that was when I was declared persona non grata by Region Three of the Central Luzon NBI."

"What? Why did the Philippine National Bureau of Investigation declare you unwelcome?" asked Ross.

Emanuel smiled and scratched his head.

"Well sir, it had something to do with that night outside the lighthouse in Olongapo, I believe. Remember?"

"Oh, I see," said Ross.

"But then Lailani told me her husband Lars was taking her to Switzerland to startup a new restaurant. They agreed to sponsor me, and so…here I am," said Emanuel beaming.

"Well, I'll be damned," said Ross.

Emanuel cocked his head to one side and squinted his eyes.

"Maybe you won't, sir."

Ross looked at the handkerchief in Emanuel's left hand. It was the same one Ross had given him in Manila.

"I see you still have that old thing," noted Ross.

Emanuel folded the handkerchief and shoved it into his parka pocket.

"Yes. It's been around a little bit."

Emanuel pressed a black plastic remote control keychain in his hand and the Mercedes-Benz trunk automatically popped open. He picked up Ross's suitcase and placed it into the opened trunk. Then he slammed the trunk lid down.

Thump.

Ross opened the front passenger door and sat down. He located the seat belt and buckled himself in. A beautiful aroma of roses immediately overtook him.

Emanuel with his car fresheners again, he thought.

Emanuel had left the Mercedes-Benz engine running with the heater on. The interior of the car was a warm respite from the cold.

Emanuel's taxi was a 1972 Mercedes-Benz S-Class. It was a four door luxury sedan which had a 6.9 liter V-8 engine, anti-lock brakes, self-leveling heavy duty suspension, black leather seats, six-CD changer, Sirius satellite radio, and GPS system. The exterior color was a high gloss black. Miniature Swiss national flags were flapping from each side of the front bumper.

I feel like a visiting head of state from a third world country, thought Ross.

Emanuel climbed into the Mercedes-Benz and put on his seat belt. He gently slid the forty-one year old key into the ignition and started the engine. Turning his head left and then right, Emanuel scanned the scene before expertly pulling out into the traffic flow.

"So where did you pick up this car from, Emanuel?" asked Ross.

"Oh, this car came from my cousin's husband. He's a really nice guy. You know, they sponsored me and brought me over here. They paid my bills, and even let me live in their attic. So, I told them I could pay them back, if I could just get my foot in the door somewhere. Well, Lars loaned me this car, and set me up in the taxi business here."

"It's a small world all right. But, whatever happened to your Albatross plane?" asked Ross.

"Oh, that got confiscated by NPI I'm afraid to say, sir," said Emanuel.

Ross frowned.

"I'm really sorry to hear that, Emanuel. But isn't it amazing how we meet again?" asked Ross.

Emanuel smiled.

"Yes sir, it is. It is quite amazing. But then again, I hang out at the airport everyday looking for fares. The airport is the best place to pick up the really fascinating people. Yes sir, you never know what adventures the airport has in store for you any single day."

Emanuel took a quick glance at the traffic in his side mirror.

"So where are we off to, sir?"

"The Hotel Bristol," instructed Ross.

"Yes sir."

The Hotel Bristol is a favorite of tourists, businessmen, and intelligence operators.

Nestled within the middle Zurich cultural hub, the Hotel Bristol is only ten kilometers north from the airport. It's close to the Central Zurich Hauptbahnhof Station, tram and bus stops, and is near the world-class shopping of the Bahnhofstrasse. The gorgeous scenic surrounding area is resplendent with museums, theater, opera, restaurants, cafes and clubs.

The Bristol has a classical style about it, and is only a twenty minute walk from beautiful Lake Zurich. It's well known for having a twenty-four hour concierge desk which can supply just about anything and everything, at anytime.

Ross knew he would make good use of the free Wi-Fi internet, business center, and guarded lobby safes. Unlike room safes which were unobserved most of the day, the lobby safes were constantly under surveillance by the professional security conscious concierge staff.

The temperature this time of year in Zurich was cold, colder, and coldest. Snow was coming down in large frolicking flakes everywhere outside. Ross marveled at how clear the autobahn was though. Swiss government administrators were meticulous when it came to snow removal projects.

Emanuel used the travel time for some small talk.

"Tell me sir, since the last time I saw you in the Philippines, whatever happened to Miss Lin?"

Ross deliberated for a moment, and then responded.

"She and I kept in touch. It's hard to maintain a long distance relationship when I'm in America and she's in Malaysia."

"Yes sir, I'm sure it is. But do you think your paths will cross again, sir?"

"Emanuel, it's funny you should ask that, because she emailed me before I left, and she is in fact coming over here."

"How's that, sir?"

"Well, it seems her old boss is here, and she notified him that she was going to take some vacation time, and she's using him as a reference so to speak for the trip."

"Oh, I see sir," said Emanuel. "When will Miss Lin be here?"

"Tomorrow," Ross said looking at his Benrus, "well, actually today. She emailed me that she would be here today."

Emanuel straightened up in his seat.

"Sir?"

"Yeah?"

"You're not planning on killing a bunch of people again like you did in Olongapo, are you?"

"What?" said a startled Ross. "Of course not, Emanuel. I'm here strictly to get information only. I can assure you this will be like a pleasant vacation for me too."

"Oh, okay sir. I'm relieved to know that. I mean, I'm already persona non grata in the Philippines. I wouldn't want that to happen here."

Ross said, "You crack me up, Emanuel."

"Yes sir, crack up, thank you sir," said a smiling Emanuel.

Emanuel turned off the autobahn and was soon on Weinbergstrasse. A few kilometers more, and he turned right onto Stampfenbachstrasse. He started carefully scanning the street looking for number thirty-four. A quick right turn, and they were in front of the hotel.

"Here we are, sir," said Emanuel, "the Hotel Bristol."

Emanuel placed the Mercedes-Benz in park, and left the motor running. He got out and ran around to open the trunk.

Ross got out of the passenger side. He stretched his arms over his head and yawned.

Emanuel came around to the front with Ross's bag.

"Here we are sir," said Emanuel as he motioned to the front entrance. "Follow me."

"Aren't you afraid someone could steal your car with the motor running?" asked Ross.

"This isn't Manila, sir. After all, where would they go?" asked Emanuel smiling.

"I guess you've got a point there, Emanuel," said Ross.

The main doors electronically hissed open. Ross, with Emanuel by his side, walked into the lobby heading straight for the reception desk.

Waiting behind the main counter for them was the smiling receptionist.

The receptionist was in her middle twenties. She was tall at five feet ten inches. Her silky blonde hair hung to her shoulders with a curl on the ends. It was parted on the left side with Bettie Page type retro bangs down her forehead to her eyebrows. Her bright blue inquisitive eyes accented her already gorgeous facial features. She had a touch of blush powder on her cheeks, and wore black lipstick and black nail polish. Her lips were soft and full, and bloomed like a rose when she released her breathless voice. Her hourglass body was poured into a black satin jumpsuit that zippered in the front from the crotch to the neck. Her legs were accented by six inch heeled, black leather, knee length boots with large silver buckles at the top. A plastic nametag on her left breast proclaimed her name to be Saskia.

"Guten tag, mein Herr," said Saskia. "How may I help you?"

Ross pulled out his black diplomatic passport and handed it to Saskia.

"Hello, my name's James Ross. You should have a reservation for me."

Saskia opened the passport and quickly glanced at the customs entrance stamping, and then handed the document back to Ross.

She clicked a dozen keys on the Toshiba laptop computer in front of her.

"Let me see. Yes sir, here it is — reservation for James Ross, a standard room with single bed. You'll be in room one twenty-six on the third floor."

Saskia looked into Ross's dark brown eyes.

"That's in the rear of the hotel. It's quieter back there," she revealed.

"That's good," said Ross.

"Yes sir, your room is ready. How will you be paying today, sir?"

Ross pulled out his wallet and withdrew his blue Bank of America GSA Visa government credit card. He handed it to Saskia.

Saskia pressed more keys and entered Ross's credit card information into the computer. She gently handed the card back to Ross.

"I'll have the porter get your luggage and take you right up, Mister Ross. Is there anything else I can help you with?"

"No, I think that does it," said Ross.

Ross turned around to Emanuel.

"Emanuel, I would like to keep in touch with you while I'm here."

Emanuel reached into his pocket and pulled out an embossed business card.

"I was hoping you'd say that, sir. My number's on the card. You can reach me day or night. I'm available, and you know I'm discrete. I'll give you the best rate in Zurich."

"Thanks. I know you will."

Ross reached into his right front trousers pocket and pulled out a US hundred dollar bill.

"Here, this is for you."

Emanuel took the bill and looked at it. He folded it in half and shoved it into his faded blue jeans pocket.

"I'll keep this as a deposit, sir. I figure I own you a couple days driving for it."

"Thanks Emanuel. I'll call you."

Ross offered his hand to Emanuel.

"Yes sir, anytime."

Emanuel reached out and shook hands with Ross.

Quietly, Emanuel turned around and walked out of the hotel and into the darkness of the blistery cold Zurich night.

A middle aged porter arrived and picked up Ross's suitcase.

"Follow me sir."

Ross followed the porter to a bank of elevators.

The porter pressed the "UP" button and the elevator doors hissed open. He selected the third floor button on the control panel and looked at Ross.

"Will you be staying with us long, sir?" inquired the porter.

"Perhaps a few weeks," said Ross.

The elevator stopped at the third floor and the doors slid open.

Ross followed the porter down the long expanse of plush red carpeted hallway to room 126.

The porter slipped the electronic coded plastic keycard into its slot. The small door lock light turned from red to green.

Click.

Pulling the card out, the porter opened the door and gave Ross a tour of the room.

"We have great services available here at the Bristol, sir," said the porter. "Secure computer access, guarded safety deposit boxes, airport transfers, laundry service, twenty-four hour tour services, daily continental breakfast, and fantastic business rooms."

The porter was smiling now.

"Just about everything you could possibly need, sir," beamed the porter.

Ross said, "Thank you."

"I'm sure you will find this quite comfortable sir," said the porter. He walked to the desk and placed two electronic keyless entry cards next to the phone for Ross.

This time Ross reached into his left front trousers pocket and pulled out a folded ten Franc Swiss note. He handed it to the porter.

"Danke," said Ross.

The porter took the note and pocketed it.

"Sie sind herzlich willkommen," replied the porter.

The porter turned around and left the room, closing the door behind him.

Ross walked over and locked the door with the deadbolt. He turned around and picked up his suitcase. Then he walked over to the room's complimentary computer access desk and laid his bag at the foot of it.

Ross unzipped his bag and pulled out the charging unit for his government issued Blackberry smartphone. Noticing a bank of electric outlets on the desk near the landline phone, Ross plugged in the Blackberry and powered it up.

Soon the free Wi-Fi internet access symbol appeared on the smartphone screen.

Ross utilized and accessed the Department of Defense Secret Internet Protocol Router Network to send his emails.

He needed to let his boss know he had arrived safely, so he typed a personal encrypted email to Colonel Winbolt:

Sir,
Arrived Zurich midnight local time.
No current issues to report.
Updates will follow.
V/r
CPT James B. Ross

That was enough for now, thought Ross.

He pressed the send button and the message was transmitted through secure SIPRNET channels.

Ross placed the smartphone down on the desktop and allowed it to continue charging.

He picked up the receiver of the nightstand phone and pressed the wakeup service button.

Ross asked for a wakeup call at seven o'clock in the morning.

The soft demure voice of the female receptionist purred, "Certainly sir, have a pleasant evening Mister Ross."

"Thank you, ma'am," replied Ross.

Ross laid the receiver back in its cradle.

He didn't really need the wakeup call.

Ever since he had attended the Special Forces Qualification Course at Fort Bragg, he could just somehow *will* his body to wake up at anytime. It wasn't magical. It was just something that many SF soldiers were capable of doing.

Ross hung his black suit in the closet, and stowed the rest of his clothes in the drawers of the dresser below the widescreen Sony television.

He walked into the bathroom and stripped off his travel clothes, throwing them down.

Ross loaded his toothbrush with hotel courtesy toothpaste, and methodically brushed the staleness of many hours worth of travel out of his mouth.

Glancing in the mirror and fingering the stubble on his chin, Ross decided to shave in the morning.

He walked over and slid open the twin transparent glass doors of the shower stall and stepped in.

Pulling the crystal power jet handles outward, he straightened out his arms and leaned forward, pressing both of his palms against the shower wall under the needling spray. Slowly, he lowered his head and allowed the heavy stream of pulsating hot water to cascade over his aching body.

Ross completed the shower in his usual four minutes. He grabbed one of the large green terrycloth towels and dried himself off. Then he put on a pair of red plaid boxer shorts, and crawled under the bed sheets.

Ross immediately fell into a deep luxurious sleep.

Thump!

Thump!

Thump!

Thump!

Someone was knocking on Ross's hotel room door.

He squinted at the luminescent tritium dial of his Benrus.

It's two o'clock in the morning.

Ross shook the cobwebs from his head and stumbled out of bed.

He walked over to the door in his red plaid boxer shorts, and peered through the security viewfinder.

It was Lin.

CHAPTER SEVEN

DIE GLOCKE

I don't feel right.

I just don't feel right at all, thought Wolfram von Lugoff to himself.

He had that feeling that people get right before they have a heart attack, or cardiac arrest.

It was an indescribable feeling of overall malaise.

Doctors all over the world were well aware of any patient coming in and uttering those infamous words: *I just don't feel right.*

Lugoff was lying down on a surplus Wehrmacht military cot in his Talstrasse warehouse.

He closed his eyes tightly.

His thoughts were spinning, and he felt as though he would lose consciousness at any second.

Oh God I've got to stay awake, he thought.

If I fall asleep I may never wakeup.

But succumb he did.

Lugoff drifted off to that land between consciousness and unconsciousness —

— between life and death —

— between reality and dreams.

Lugoff's body was suffering the aftereffects of immediate systemic dematerialization, and intrinsic spontaneous cell regeneration.

That's what time travel does to you.

His mind drifted forward into subconscious thought.

Just a little more than an hour ago, he had run his third systems check on the machine that Heinrich Himmler had nicknamed Die Glocke.

All systems on the seventy year old apparatus checked out okay.

So, Lugoff decided to put the mechanism to a test run.

The single entrance-escape hatch on the capsule was closed and secured.

He reclined back in the contoured Luftwaffe pilot seat.

Next, he buckled himself into the Fallschirmjager harness.

He looked at the stainless steel Blancpain chronograph on his left wrist and noted the time.

Midnight.

Not really knowing what to expect, Lugoff powered up the equipment.

He saw the Macht Auf gauge start to glow an ancient yellow luminescence.

Yellow always means yield.

I wonder if I should press on?

Then any vestiges of lingering doubt evaporated from Lugoff's mind.

Of course.

I must.

Lugoff had both hands on the cold metal of the Gangschaltung control lever.

He pressed the Trolit Thermoplast button on top, and ratcheted the lever backward.

Clack, clack, clack.

The sounds coincided with the spinning of the control panel mechanical sprocket calendar.

Clack, clack, clack.

If Lugoff could have seen the outside of Die Glocke, he would have been amazed.

The base of the machine was emitting a greenish-orange glow, and the entire outer capsule was starting to vibrate slightly.

The clacking sound inside was in competition to a swirling, rushing, windstorm sound growing in intensity outside.

Inside Die Glocke, Lugoff's body was immediately flushed with an overwhelming sense of peaceful bliss.

He hadn't realized that he had closed his eyes, but when he opened them, he was staring at the control panel mechanical sprocket calendar.

Its day-month-year dial was wildly spinning backwards.

...27-MAR-2011...

...19-OCT-1989...

...21-JAN-1961...

...01-SEP-1939...

...15-APR-1912...

Lugoff pushed the Gangschaltung control lever forward, and watched the calendar dial come to an abrupt stop.

It stopped on 31 July 1900.

My God, he thought.

The blissful feeling Lugoff had experienced was suddenly replaced with a dull throbbing headache.

He unbuckled himself and sat upright.

He started to feel sick seasick.

But then, almost immediately, the feeling started to subside.

Reaching forward, he spun the circular handle on the escape hatch counterclockwise until it stopped.

Anxiously, Lugoff placed both hands on the hatch and pushed forward.

His ears popped as a distinct hissing sound, reminiscent of a submarine lockout chamber, filled the capsule as soon as the seal was broken to the outside world.

And what a world it was.

Lugoff climbed outside Die Glocke on wobbly legs.

He gained his composure, and stared into the darkness.

Using his cell phone as a flashlight, Lugoff looked around in wonderment.

The Talstrasse warehouse was completely gone.

It no longer existed now.

It did not exist in the year 1900.

The space where it existed had changed.

Time changes space.

Lugoff and Die Glocke were now situated in a farmer's field of potatoes.

A muddy field.

There was a slight fog misting about, and the foreboding hue of the night sky was illuminated by an eerie moon, making the whole scene reminiscent of a macabre Edgar Allan Poe tale.

His attention was caught by some lights off in the distance.

Lugoff squinted his eyes and could make out what appeared to be a building about fifty meters or so to his front.

I must find out what that is, he thought.

Giving in to his own scientific curiosity, Lugoff placed one foot in front of the other and slogged forward through the muddy field towards the lights.

As he walked forward, Lugoff could see that the building was some type of pub or tavern.

A weathered wooden sign above the entrance read simply: *Bierstube.*

Pocketing his cell phone, Lugoff approached cautiously.

Wooden shutters were folded back on the sides of the windows, allowing the warm glow of a fire lit space to welcome him as he approached.

The front door was open, but before entering, Lugoff stomped his feet and attempted to wipe the mud off them on the entrance doormat.

He unintentionally held his breath as he walked through the doorway.

The tavern had six wooden tables spread about, with patrons sitting at most of them. There was a large wooden bar counter to the rear, with bar stools strewn about in front of it. The bar counter had a brass boot railing encircling its bottom, with spittoons ingloriously gracing each end. A huge framed mirror adorned the wall behind the bar, with bottles of liquor and drinking glasses stacked in front of it. Beer taps displaying emblems of local brews were situated behind the top of the counter. To the left of the bar was a huge stone fireplace with the glowing remnants of the evenings' coals. Hanging from the ceiling by a chain was what looked like an oxcart wheel with lighted lanterns dangling from every spoke.

Lugoff was approached by a large, burly, middle-aged man who looked like he could plow a field without a horse.

"Guten Abend. May I help you?" asked the owner while wiping off his hands with a dish towel.

Lugoff snapped out of his daze and took a breath.

"Um, yes. May I have a drink please?"

The owner looked at Lugoff curiously while continuing to wipe his hands.

"Ja. Do you want to sit at the bar or a table, mein Herr?"

"Ah, the bar please," replied Lugoff.

"Good. Come with me," said the owner, who happened to also be the bartender.

Lugoff followed the man to the bar and situated himself on a wooden stool.

"Now, what would you like, mein Herr?"

Lugoff looked at the liquor bottles and then saw the beer taps.

"Just a beer please."

The owner flipped the dish towel onto his right shoulder.

"What kind of beer?"

Lugoff pointed to the closest beer tap.

"That one."

The owner carefully filled a glass with beer and placed it in front of Lugoff.

"Anything else?" asked the owner.

Lugoff thought a moment.

"Do you happen to have today's newspaper?"

Without saying a word, the owner reached down behind the bar and came up with a folded newspaper. He slapped it down on the wet countertop in front of Lugoff.

"Enjoy," said the owner.

"Danke," replied Lugoff.

Lugoff picked up the newspaper and unfolded it.

He scanned the top right hand corner and noted the date.

July 31, 1900.

Good Lord, thought Lugoff.

The headline read: *KAISER COMPARES GERMANS TO HUNS.*

Lugoff read through the article and saw that it was written about a speech given by Kaiser Wilhelm II on 27 July.

Lugoff remembered learning about the speech from his high school history lessons.

It was the famous *Huns Speech* given as Kaiser Wilhelm II dispatched German troops to fight in China. The Kaiser referenced how history remembered the brave battles which the Huns fought a thousand years ago, and how the Chinese would today remember the bravery of the Germans for a future thousand years.

My God, thought Lugoff.

Die Glocke works!

I really am back in time!

I have traveled into the fourth dimension!

Lugoff put the newspaper down and picked up his beer. He downed it in three long gulps.

The bartender reached over and refilled his glass.

Oh damn. I have Swiss Francs in my wallet and some coins in my pockets. But they're all from the future!

The owner started wiping down the countertop with his dish towel while staring at Lugoff.

With a serious face, Lugoff reached in his back pocket and took out his wallet.

He pulled out a five Swiss Franc banknote and folded it in half to try to conceal its future-looking appearance. Then he pulled all the silver coins out of his trousers pockets and placed them on top of the banknote on the countertop.

Lugoff hoped the midnight hours, dim lighting, and alcohol would aid in camouflaging his future money.

"Keep the change," said Lugoff pleasantly.

The tavern owner's face suddenly broke into a smile. Without looking at the currency, he brought up a cigar box from behind the bar and scooped all of the money off of the countertop and into it.

"Danke," said the owner.

The deception worked.

Lugoff hurriedly drank down his second beer and stood up.

"Gute nacht," said Lugoff as he turned and headed for the door.

“Come back again, mein Herr,” replied the bar owner while closing the lid of the cigar box.

Lugoff hurriedly slogged through the mud and back to his machine.

Once he was inside, he strapped himself in and powered up Die Glocke. He very methodically set the mechanical sprocket calendar to the present day.

Lugoff pressed the Trolit Thermoplast button and ratcheted the Gangschaltung control lever forward.

Soon he was hurtling forward through time, which Lugoff now knew altered space as well.

Lugoff looked at his Blancpain chronograph timepiece.

Midnight.

It's still only midnight, he thought.

Now he was back on the war surplus cot and staring at the corrugated metal ceiling of the Talstrasse warehouse.

His headache was gone, and he was starting to feel better overall.

Within seconds he collapsed into a deep sleep.

His dreams were filled with visions of demons tormenting him… and tearing him asunder.

PART TWO

The only way to win a war is to prevent it.

George C. Marshall
1880 — 1959
US Army General
Nobel Peace Prize 1953

CHAPTER EIGHT

WELCOME ALLIES

Ross was on his left side sleeping soundly. His right arm was around Lin's waist, and his face was buried in her hair.

They were sleeping like spoons.

Bringgg!

Bringggg!

Bringgggg!

The ringing of the hotel courtesy telephone jarred Ross awake.

He reached out and snatched up the receiver.

On the other side of the connection was a pleasant female voice.

"Good morning, Mister Ross. This is your seven a.m. wakeup call."

"Thank you," replied Ross.

"My pleasure, sir."

Ross dropped the receiver into its cradle.

He turned his head and looked at Lin.

Lin had rolled over onto her back. She stretched both of her arms up towards the headboard. The covers had fallen down to just below her navel. The softness of her skin was in direct contrast to the hardness of her erect nipples pointing upwards.

Lin's nude body teased at him.

Ross was immediately reminded of the beautiful *"Sleeping Bather"* nineteenth century painting by Pierre-Auguste Renoir. He had studied the great painters in an electives art course years ago while attending Texas Christian University.

He couldn't help but smile.

I must be in heaven.

My God, she's beautiful.

She's all I want in this life.

I wish this moment would last forever.

But Ross knew he had a mission to do.

He had to get on it.

Ross leaned over and gently kissed Lin on her soft lips.

Her scent intoxicated him.

His chest brushed across her nipples, further adding fuel to his already consuming desire.

"Good morning, Lin."

Lin smiled and her eyelids fluttered open.

"Good morning, handsome."

Lin reached out and wrapped her arms around Ross's neck.

She pulled him close and kissed him wantonly on the lips.

Ross's defenses waned and he fell under her magical spell.

Lin's luxuriously sensuous body folded together perfectly with Ross's muscled torso.

She smiled and played with Ross's hair for a few seconds, twisting and turning it in her fingers. She tried to brush it off his forehead, but it just fell back down again only in more disarray.

Ross stiffened, and Lin threw her head back while arching her back.

She blossomed around Ross and opened herself fully to him, while pressing back on Ross's chest with both of her hands.

Lin smiled at Ross now, and allowed him to envelope her —

— to overcome her —

— to seduce her —

— to love her.

Lin held on tight as Ross kissed her long —

— and slow —

— and tenderly.

Lin closed her eyes and clutched Ross, hoping the moment would never end.

Their movements flowed like a powerful current in the sea, ever smoothly and increasing, until the undulations of the swell crested and crashed into the shore in all its majesty.

One hour later, Ross was in his black suit, and Lin was looking very pretty in a stylish Alfred Angelo pleated red dress. They were downstairs and enjoying the Hotel Bristol's extravagant breakfast cuisine.

"… and can you believe that Emanuel is here?" said Ross.

Lin smiled.

"I *can* actually believe that. He's quite the interesting fellow…and a good friend."

"Yeah," said Ross.

Ross picked up his cup and took a sip of Nestle dark roast coffee.

"Lin, I need to get over to the US Consular Agency this morning and pick up a car from them. Why don't we go together?"

Lin had a mouthful of blueberry muffin and hurriedly washed it down with a gulp of orange juice.

"Ah, um, I'm supposed to meet Mister Watlington at noon today for lunch. I emailed him before I left, and he told me that he would assist me in any way he can."

Lin's expression became troubled.

"Of course, I only told him I was coming here on vacation. He knows nothing about my dreams or you being here."

Ross thought for a few seconds.

"I wonder if Mister Watlington would mind if I came to lunch with you guys. My office has already notified him about my trip, as a courtesy. I could use his assistance as well. He's pretty well connected in all the embassy circles. He could be a welcome ally."

Lin said, "I'm sure you can. I'm positive he'll help you out in every way he can, once you explain things to him."

Ross nodded affirmatively.

"Where are you meeting him for lunch?" asked Ross.

Lin said, "At someplace called the Reindeer Beer Hall, on Niederdorfstrasse or something."

Ross pulled out his Blackberry.

"Wait a minute," he said.

He did a quick Google search.

"That wouldn't be the Rheinfelder Bierhalle on Niederdorfstrasse by any chance, would it?"

Lin took out her cell phone and rechecked her messages.

"Yep, that's it."

Ross said, "Okay, well I could meet you guys there after I pick up the car. What do you think?"

"That sounds good, James."

"Okay."

Ross pulled out Emanuel's business card and gave it to Lin. He had already placed Emanuel's phone number into his cell phone contact list.

"Here Lin, take this. I've got Emanuel coming over here to take me to pick up my car. You should ask him to drive you to lunch."

"Okay, thanks."

Ross glanced at the check.

He wrote his room number on the bill and left a ten Swiss Franc tip.

Ross and Lin left the breakfast bar and walked to the hotel main entrance.

Ross reached into his pocket and pulled out a plastic keycard.

"Here's the room key, Lin. I'll give you a call when I'm done and on my way."

"Okay."

Ross leaned over and kissed Lin lightly on the lips.

The hotel receptionist, Saskia, smiled pleasantly as she watched the scene unfold.

Forty minutes later, Emanuel dropped Ross off at a nondescript, gray stone, four story, governmental building on Dufourstrasse.

The American Consular Agency was located on the third floor of 101 Dufourstrasse. It's a smaller consulate, which mostly deals with passport entry and exit visa requirements for US citizens. The staff also provides excellent local threat warnings, and gives out travel advisory and local traffic information.

Ross was set to meet with a Foreign Service Specialist General Services Officer to sign out a vehicle. That was fancy talk to say he was signing out a car from the quartermaster supply officer.

Lorrie Andrea was waiting for him.

"Good morning, Captain Ross," said Lorrie.

Lorrie Andrea was twenty-eight years old. Her chocolate brown hair was cut with a short-and-sassy type look that gave her a fresh, clean, and exuberantly vibrant appearance. She walked and talked with an air of authority that she developed from the four years she had spent as a United States Marine.

Lorrie had wire-rimmed glasses perched on the end of her nose, which gave her beautiful face an even cuter look. She wore no makeup, except some very glistening lip gloss. She was dressed in tight black jeans, which were secured with a narrow silver plated western cowboy belt. She also wore a long sleeved, open collared black shirt, with white buttons up the front. Her feet were nestled into coco brown leather cowboy boots. Just shy of five feet eleven inches tall and weighing one hundred and forty pounds, her figure was trim and fit, and she knew it.

Lorrie smiled and thrust out her hand to Ross.

"Good morning," said Ross as he shook Lorrie's hand.

"I've got your car all ready for you down in the basement motor pool. I'll walk you down there so you can inspect it before you sign for it."

"Sounds good," agreed Ross.

Lorrie did not take Ross to the elevators. She led him to the stairwell instead.

"This is how I get my daily exercise," explained Lorrie.

Ross smiled.

"I see."

Lorrie escorted Ross down the narrow twisty serpentine staircase.

They arrived at the basement, and Lorrie led Ross through a row of mesh wire property cages lined to the ceiling. The cages contained every conceivable type of supply a consulate could need, everything from mops to computers.

"We keep the vehicles down here most of the time so they don't freeze up," said Lorrie.

Ross followed Lorrie around a corner which opened up to reveal a vast underground warehouse where eight government sedans were parked.

She led Ross over to a 2013 Ford Mondeo.

Parent car companies sometimes change the names of models of their vehicles for the overseas market. A famous example of this was years ago, when Nissan Motors Limited in Japan marketed their Nissan Fairlady model in the United States as the Datsun 280ZX.

The Ford Mondeo is what the Ford Fusion is known as in Europe.

Many think the story of the 2013 redesigned Ford Mondeo/Fusion begins in Great Britain.

Aston Martin was owned by the Ford Motor Company from 1994 until 2007. Ford still retains ten percent of Aston Martin to this day. It's rumored that the designer of the Aston Martin Rapide also designed the 2013 Ford Fusion, known as the Ford Mondeo in Europe. Both cars look very similar, especially around the front grill area. Both cars are available with a Ford Duratec engine. The Aston Martin line utilizes the Duratec 6.0 liter V-12 engine, while the Fusion is available with a multitude of engine choices, including the Duratec. There was even a rumor that the Aston Martin V-12 engine was simply two Ford V-6 Duratec engines linked together. Of course this was not true, but it made for interesting speculation. However, the fact that Aston Martin redesigned the front grill area of their new 2013 Rapide does give one reason to ponder the possibilities.

Ross preferred naturally aspirated internal combustion engines, like the Duratec, over complicated turbine engines. He always felt simpler was more dependable.

The Ford Mondeo/Fusion was the perfect balance of European elegance and American enterprise.

"Here's your vehicle Captain Ross. You're getting this Ford Mondeo."

The car was a 2013 model in sterling gray, with the steering wheel on the right hand side. It had the usual bells and whistles, but under its hood was something very popular in Europe: a Duratec 3.5 liter 263 horsepower V-6 engine.

"Where do I sign?" asked Ross.

Lorrie placed the government hand receipt on the hood of the car for Ross. He wrote his name and date on it, and handed the document back.

"Thanks. I'll take good care of it."

Lorrie smiled and handed Ross the keys and her business card.

"I know you will," she said.

Ross looked around.

"So how do I get out of here?"

Lorrie pointed with her right index finger to the far wall.

"Over there is the exit."

She extracted her cell phone from its belt pouch and did some scrolling. Then she pressed a button.

The far wall started to creak and groan, and then mechanically cranked up and slowly slid itself underneath the basement ceiling.

The wall was actually a cleverly disguised automatic double garage door.

"Just go out through that exit. Take a left and you'll be on Dufourstrasse."

"Okay, and thanks," said Ross.

Ross clicked the automatic door opener on the keychain.

A series of tiny red warning lights came on around the vehicle, and then the doors unlocked.

Ross opened the drivers' door and sat down inside.

He pressed another button on the keychain and the ignition key flipped out like a switchblade knife.

Ross slid the key into the ignition switch and turned it to the right.

The engine came on, as well as a multitude of blue illuminated dashboard lights.

He checked to make sure the emergency brake was off, buckled himself in, and took a glance into his rearview mirror for safety.

Ross depressed the black button on the automatic shifter and eased the transmission into drive.

Turning his head to the right, Ross gave a final wave of his hand to Lorrie Andrea.

He slowly drove the Mondeo through the underground garage exit and out into the Dufourstrasse winter wonderland.

Ross was happy with the way the car was handling in the snow and ice. The V-6 263 horsepower engine was giving him the power needed to churn through the sludge and sleet. The seventeen inch aluminum wheels with Dunlop Winter Sport tires were gripping the road as well as could be expected.

Ross glanced at his Benrus.

It's only nine-thirty. I have time to check out the Swiss National Bank, he thought to himself.

Ross scrolled up the Global Positioning System on his Blackberry. He had already added the address of the Swiss National Bank to his GPS under the abbreviation of *SNB*.

Ross drove the Mondeo following the instructions given by the GPS.

In thirty-five minutes he was parked outside Börsenstrasse 15.

Ross locked the Mondeo and walked across the street.

It looks like it's built out of granite, he thought.

The exterior of the Swiss National Bank was a grand affair resembling more of a museum or opera house than a bank. Hand pruned trees and shrubs ringed the perimeter. The first floor windows had decorative iron security grates enclosing them. Some of the upper story windows were the type that could be opened, complete with balconies, potted plants, and shutters. There were several hand-carved statues of historical figures on the fourth floor balcony overlooking the huge fountains of the front mall area below. You got the feeling that these larger-than-life effigies of the Swiss founding fathers were a monument to safeguarding the resources within. The entrance door was at least twelve feet tall, and looked like it was constructed out of iron and lacquered mahogany.

Ross entered the lobby of the institution.

Extravagant elegance is the best way to describe the lobby of the Swiss National Bank. It represented the best of German architecture and French style. The lobby was resplendent with domed ceilings, crystal chandeliers, marble floors, mahogany counters, oak chairs, vintage tapestries, and antique paintings. There were also overhead stock exchange screen monitors, Wi-Fi computer access, security cameras, concierges, receptionists, guides, armed guards, and a coffee shop with strudel.

I'm not in Kansas anymore, thought Ross.

Ross slowly sauntered over to the coffee shop area.

"What may I get for you, sir?" asked the waitress dressed in a very professional looking business suit.

Ross looked at the offerings.

There was everything from espresso to Vienna sausages.

"Um, let me try a medium café macchiato, please."

The waitress smiled.

"Yes, very good sir."

"Um, and let me have one of those swirly iced strudels too."

"Yes, of course sir."

"You don't by chance have onion soup, do you?"

The waitress blushed.

"Um, no sir, we don't."

"Oh, okay," said Ross.

Ross gathered his coffee and strudel. He looked around for a seat that would give him unbridled surveillance of the lobby, but remain inconspicuous. He finally sat down in a chair at the far end of the coffee shop.

Ross carefully took in his surroundings.

Patrons were everywhere conducting business. Ross got the impression that he was watching the rotors turn on a fine Swiss chronometer. He pulled out his Blackberry and pretended to be conducting some business online while he continued his reconnaissance of the scene.

Thirty minutes passed and Ross needed to stretch.

It's time to use the restroom ruse.

Ross got up, tossed his empty Styrofoam cup and strudel wrapper into a wastebasket, and walked into the men's room. Inside was a shoeshine valet.

Why not?

Ross settled back in a tall chair and allowed the man to go to work polishing his shoe leather. He was impressed as his well-worn black shoes took on a new lustrous appearance. He tipped the man graciously and exited back into the lobby.

One more coffee and then I'll have to leave, thought Ross.

He walked back to the coffee shop and ordered. With a fresh cup of steaming coffee in his hands, Ross took a seat and continued his reconnaissance of the inner workings of the Swiss National Bank.

Well, that's interesting.

As Ross was sipping his coffee, he observed the Honorable Simon Watlington standing at one of the teller counters.

How odd.

He must have come in while I was in the restroom, thought Ross.

Standing right next to Watlington were three men.

They were all in their late twenties or early thirties, and well-dressed in suits and ties.

The men had dark complexions and appeared to be of Middle Eastern descent.

Afghani, thought Ross.

Or possibly Pakistani.

Watlington and the three men appeared to be chatting innocently. Then they shook hands, and all three walked together to the main entrance and exited.

Ross got up and casually strolled over to the front windows where he could observe the foursome without being detected.

There was a black Audi A8 sedan parked in the front with its trunk open. Two male uniformed bank employees stood beside the trunk unloading a dolly. The employees were both armed with flap holstered pistols on their hips. They appeared to be loading a small wooden footlocker into the trunk. The employees strained as they lifted it, but successfully placed it into the trunk, and then slammed the lid shut.

All four of the men then got into the Audi, with Watlington sitting in the front passenger seat.

The Audi A8 sedan slowly pulled away from the curb and headed out towards the traffic. It was soon swallowed up into the flow.

Ross let out a slow whistle from between his lips.

CHAPTER NINE

FATE FOR LUNCH

Ross utilized his GPS and drove straight to number seventy-six Niederdorfstrasse to the Rheinfelder Bierhalle for his lunch rendezvous.

He parked the Ford Mondeo across the street and walked inside.

The maitre d' escorted Ross to Lin's table.

"Hello Lin," said Ross.

Lin waved for Ross to sit down next to her.

"Hi. How are you? Did you pick up your car?"

"Yeah, it's a nice one too, a brand new Ford Mondeo."

Ross casually surveyed the room.

"So, Mister Watlington isn't here yet?"

Lin shook her head.

"Nope. Not yet."

Ross picked up a menu and opened it.

"Well, let's see what's good here."

Ross scanned the menu.

"It looks like the special is schnitzel cordon bleu. What do you think, Lin?"

Lin peered at the menu in Ross's hands.

"What's schnitzel?" asked Lin.

Ross explained, "Schnitzel's a thin, tenderized, boneless meat, that's breaded with flour. It can be any type of meat, such as beef, pork, or whatever. They call it cordon bleu when they wrap it around a slice of ham and cheese, and either bake or fry it. In French, the words *cordon bleu* translates to mean *blue ribbon.*"

"That sounds really good," she said.

Lin's eyes casually drifted to the restaurant entrance.

"And it looks like Mister Watlington has just arrived."

Lin nodded her head in the direction of the entrance.

Simon Watlington had indeed just arrived, and was talking with the maitre d'.

The maitre d' bowed and beckoned Watlington to follow him to Ross and Lin's table.

As Watlington approached their table he smiled broadly, and waved his hand.

"Hello, hello there. Mind if I join you?" beamed Watlington.

Ross stood up.

"Of course sir, please do."

Watlington shook hands with Ross, and then leaned over and gave Lin a friendly hug.

He pulled out a chair and sat down. Ross followed suit.

Watlington said, “It’s so good to see you both again after all this time.”

“It really is,” said Lin. “And I want to thank you so much for meeting with us, sir.”

Watlington gave his broadest smile.

“Well, no problem at all, Lin. So, how is everyone doing?”

“Fine, sir,” said Lin.

“Yes sir, really good,” chimed in Ross.

“That’s great. That’s just great. I can’t believe that fate has brought us together again.”

Lin smiled. “It’s amazing isn’t it, sir.”

Watlington shifted focus directly to Lin.

“It truly is. As you know, I retired from State and finally found my niche in life, that being teaching.”

“Why teaching, sir?” asked Lin, tapping a finger on her water glass.

“Well, I suppose that I really do love the stimulating academic environment here, and enjoy the intellectual curiosity that goes with it. I ended up teaching a class on international terrorism. And I suppose that I flatter myself by saying that I enjoy passing on my somewhat limited knowledge of terrorism to the students.”

Lin said, “Oh sir, you’re much too modest. It’s the State Departments loss that you are no longer with them, and it’s your students’ gain that you are here now.”

“Well, thank you for that, Lin. But it was time for me to retire. A man has to know when it’s time to move on.”

Watlington shifted his eyes to Ross.

"And James, I just want you to know that I'm at your disposal to aid you in any way I can."

"Thank you, sir. But I feel I may be on a wild goose chase here."

"Maybe, maybe not, time will tell," said Watlington.

Just then the waiter appeared.

"Pardon me, madame et messieurs. May I take your orders, please?" asked the waiter, as he placed water glasses on the table for Ross and Watlington.

Watlington spoke up.

"Excuse me everyone, but this restaurant is famous for its cordon bleu. May I recommend we have the schnitzel cordon bleu?"

"Yes," said Lin.

"Sounds good," said Ross smiling.

"Along with the cordon bleu, we should have their world famous fries, krautsalat, and Rekord Turbinenbau, which is a local beer on tap. That's traditional," said Watlington.

Ross looked at Lin.

"Sounds good to me," said Ross.

"Yes, me too," agreed Lin.

"Very good then," said Watlington.

Watlington looked at the waiter and nodded his head.

"An excellent choice, mein Herr," said the waiter. "You will not be disappointed, believe me."

"Um, excuse me," interrupted Ross.

"Mein Herr?" asked the waiter.

"Do you have French onion soup today?"

The waiter looked at Ross curiously.

“Ah, I’m sorry mein Herr, but we don’t. Our soup today is a very delicious potato cream. May I bring you some?” asked the waiter.

“No, that’s okay,” said a disappointed Ross.

The waiter looked at Lin and Watlington.

“I’m good, thanks,” said Lin.

“None for me either,” responded Watlington.

The waiter hurried off to the kitchen, and Watlington started up the conversation again.

“So how do you like emergency room nursing now, Lin?”

“Oh, I enjoy it really. It keeps me busy, and it’s fulfilling to help people.”

“It’s quite the jump from State Department executive personal secretary, isn’t it?” said Watlington.

Lin shifted in her seat.

“It is, but I’ll probably continue with my medical education and go to graduate school to become a physician assistant.”

“Wow, that’s wonderful. That’s really great. And will you then continue working at the Twin Towers Medical Center?”

“I’m not sure yet. We’ll see what happens.”

Watlington smiled and shifted his gaze to Ross.

“What about you, James? What’s in your future?”

Ross thought for a second and said, “Well, I enjoy what I’m doing now, and as long as I can make a difference I’ll keep at it.”

“That’s excellent, James.”

“I guess it’s meant to be,” said Ross, “like fate.”

Watlington cocked up an eyebrow.

“Ah, as the Greeks would say —*fatum,*” said Watlington.

"Something like that," replied Ross.

Watlington clasped his hands together on the table as if in benediction.

"*Fatum* can also be translated to mean destiny, or even doom. Did you know that?" asked Watlington.

"No. I didn't," said Ross.

"Indeed," replied Watlington. "Scripture says 'to run with endurance the race that is set before us.' Prophetic, isn't it?"

Ross looked perplexed.

"Um, I'm not sure I follow you, sir."

The restaurant was filling with their lunch crowd now and becoming quite boisterous. The waiter approached their table with the orders.

"Here you go, enjoy," said the waiter as he placed on their table huge plates overflowing with schnitzel cordon bleu, succulent pommes frites, creamy krautsalat, and steins foaming with ice cold beer.

Watlington shifted his gaze to somewhere between Ross and Lin. He was determined to continue his lecture.

"It means we really have no choice in the matter. Fate, destiny, doom, are all interrelated. Our fate leads to our destiny, and we thus are doomed to run the course, wherever it may lead us."

Ross's interest was piqued.

"That's interesting, sir. But I believe we can control our destiny with the decisions we make. I really don't believe that we are on some preordained fate course."

Lin could sense something was wrong with the conversation. These two men were jousting with each other. She began nervously eating her food.

Watlington said, "Fascinating, James. And how do we do that? Do you mean to say that you actually believe you can alter your destiny by making certain decisions, by choosing one way or the other?"

Ross had a piece of cordon bleu on his fork and lifted it to his mouth.

"Yes, I do."

"But what if you could live through your mistakes, and then be able to go back and correct them? Would you do it?" asked Watlington. "Would you go back into the past to correct the errors? Would you want a chance to make things right, once and for all?"

Ross thought a moment while he was munching.

"Oh, you mean like reincarnation? I suppose so."

Watlington continued probing.

"Not so much like reincarnation. I mean, what if science found a way for us to go back in time? What if we became so scientifically advanced that we could travel back, and change our destinies?"

Ross looked puzzled.

"Because time is really our most precious commodity, don't you think?" asked Watlington. "Time is more valuable than money. Time is the only real wealth."

Ross said, "In reincarnation, you have the ability to be born again and try life again. They say you have the chance to correct mistakes from past lives. But, if you're talking about actually going back and changing the past, I say no way."

Watlington was intrigued.

"Why's that?"

"Because," said Ross, "what's to stop a bad guy, like a terrorist, from going back and making things worse?"

"Oh yes," said Watlington, "I see. In a way, terrorism is much like that. It reincarnates itself over and over. I have a special block of instruction at the university on how today's radicalized Islamists are carrying on a tradition of Holy War handed down from generation to generation. Today's Jihadists are attempting to correct the fundamental mistakes of their forefathers."

Ross knew he could be treading on thin ice by engaging Watlington.

"What mistakes?" asked Ross, between bites.

Watlington explained, "The two hundred years of the Crusades, from the eleventh to the thirteenth centuries, were Christianity's attempt to rid the Holy Lands of Islamic influence. And guess what?"

Ross automatically shrugged his shoulders indicating he could not guess, as he mixed ketchup and mayonnaise together on his fries. *Too bad it's not banana ketchup,* thought Ross.

Watlington said, "The Muslims won. It's the same today. This will go on and on, unless we decide to totally eradicate the threat."

Ross said, "I understand what you're saying sir, but then again, there are Muslims who don't wage Jihad. There are Muslims who live their lives normally and peacefully like everyone else. We can't just kill them all."

"You're correct. That would be impossible. So how do we win?" asked Watlington.

Ross felt as if he had just stirred up a hornet's nest.

"Um, I guess we keep doing what we're doing, sir," replied Ross. "Putting out the brush fires before the forest catches."

With his fingers, Watlington picked up some of his French fries and dipped them into the small mayonnaise bowl.

"No," hotly retorted Watlington. "The solution is we have to pit them against each other. We have to ferment revolt and rebellion within their cells. We have to finance one group against another."

"They will destroy each other, if we give them the resources and time," Watlington said.

Ross became fascinated.

Watlington chewed on some fries.

"Look at our own country. There is downright hatred between the political parties today. The democrats and republicans despise each other. How do you think that happened?"

Ross shrugged his shoulders again.

"That toxicology was meticulously cultivated over many years. Do you think that the humongous Soviet empire simply self-destructed because of a burning desire for democracy, as the media pundits would have you believe?"

Watlington picked up his utensils and began to cut his schnitzel cordon bleu.

"No. They realized that they could not financially keep up with the arms race created by President Reagan in the eighties. So what did they do?"

Watlington chomped down on a piece of schnitzel.

Ross took the opportunity to savor some krautsalat.

"They backed off and disengaged. They decided the only way to destroy America was to let America destroy itself. Russia is winning without firing a shot."

Ross said, "That's an interesting theory, sir."

"It's more than just a theory, James," scoffed Watlington. "The population of the United States has never been more disjointed than it is now. Just look around you. There is the dichotomy between the very wealthy, and the poor. There is the permeating welfare-unemployment-food-stamp mentality of the lethargic disenfranchised. They are the new low-information populace who are angry that they couldn't make it like everybody else. So what do we do?"

"I don't know," answered Ross.

Watlington took a swig of beer and continued his dictum.

"We level the playing field even more. There is a socialist redistribution of wealth agenda slowly being revealed in our country. Take from the rich and give to the poor."

Ross knew he was adding fuel to the fire, but he wanted to see how far Watlington would take this.

"How's that, sir?" asked Ross.

Watlington had to pause a second while another mouthful of beer washed down the remnants of his mayonnaise laden French fries.

"They tax the rich into oblivion, and create a government dependent middle class. Where did that idea come from?"

Ross mumbled, "Umm …"

"It originated with Karl Marx, and was refined in Stalinist Russia," clarified Watlington.

"Oh yes," said Ross, vaguely remembering his history.

"There is a growing debate to negate the second amendment and confiscate privately owned firearms. Do you know where that idea came from?"

Ross shook his head.

"Well, it was never better implemented than in Germany by Hitler himself. You can bet an unarmed, highly taxed, indebted, lethargic and uninformed populace is exactly what our enemies want."

Watlington placed his knife and fork back down on the table.

"When the overachievers are brought down, and the underachievers are raised up, you will see a fundamental shift in United States domestic and foreign policy. You are already seeing some of it now. Remember when the Justice Department was found to be secretly confiscating the private phone records of several hundred Associated Press reporters? They were illegally intimidating the press, and they got caught. That's a violation of the first amendment to the constitution."

Watlington took another swig of beer.

Clearing his throat, Watlington said, "The Internal Revenue Service recently admitted that they selectively targeted Tea Party, Patriot, and other conservative groups who had applied for tax exempt status. The IRS delayed their applications, in some cases for years. These groups depend on receiving a tax exempt status, to allow their patrons to deduct their contributions. Otherwise, they don't receive contributions. These groups openly supported Governor Romney's campaign. Therefore, the IRS attempted to manipulate and control the outcome of our last presidential election."

Ross was stunned.

“Can you honestly tell me that the very best and brightest people our country has to offer are currently serving in the hallowed halls of government in Washington DC?” Watlington’s voice shook with conviction.

Ross contemplated, “Well …”

“Of course you can’t,” said Watlington, cutting off Ross. “They have risen on the coattails of political correctness, affirmative action, and quota theory implementation. Why, you yourself, and your beliefs, are slowly sliding into obsolescence.”

“What’s the answer then, sir?” questioned Ross.

Watlington smiled. “What the United States really needs is a benevolent dictator.”

“How’s that?” asked Ross.

Watlington was happy to explain further. “The United States needs a benevolent dictator. We need someone who is capable of extreme ruthlessness when called for, yet also capable of balanced compassion when required. Only this way will we achieve the desired result of winning a war that is at its essence a religious cultural way-of-life war, and avoid our normal uniquely unambiguous Pavlovian response cycles.”

Lin finally had enough and spoke up. “Excuse me sir, but isn’t giving everyone a chance to succeed what the United States is all about? Isn’t that what your founding fathers wished?”

As if snapped out of a trance, Watlington immediately turned his attention to Lin.

"Why, yes of course it is, Lin. It's that and much more. I was merely making an observation about how to effectively engage against a religiously radicalized enemy, that's all," said Watlington.

All three resumed eating their lunch.

Ross couldn't believe what he had just witnessed.

The tirade that Watlington had spewed forth was disconcerting at the very least.

It revealed a new side of Watlington that Ross had never seen before.

Watlington put down his fork. He looked at the young couple and smiled. Then he picked up his beer stein and raised it above his head.

"A toast," said Watlington.

Lin and Ross exchanged glances and raised their steins.

"Here's to friendship and long life," said a smiling Watlington.

Their beer steins clanged together.

Lin and Ross parroted in unison.

"To friendship and long life."

CHAPTER TEN

PAKISTANI PIPELINE

Watlington picked up the tab for the lunch. Before he left, he had promised to assist Ross in any way he could.

Lin rode with Ross in the Ford Mondeo back to the Hotel Bristol.

It was snowing again, so Ross found a parking place directly across the street from the hotel entrance.

Ross held Lin's hand as they crossed Stampfenbachstrasse and entered the hotel.

The few patrons lingering in the lobby thought Ross and Lin were just young lovers on their way to a romantic afternoon.

They talked as they rode the elevator to the third floor.

"Mister Watlington is rather strange, don't you think?" asked Lin.

Ross replied, "He's got some very strong opinions. That's for sure."

"And just before lunch, I saw him," added Ross.

"Saw him where?" asked Lin.

"At the Swiss National Bank."

"Doing what?" Lin was growing curious now.

"Yep. I saw him at the SNB with three men who I swear were Afghani, or possibly Pakistani."

"Huh? That doesn't seem right. Are you sure it was him?"

"I'm positive it was him. That's right, Lin. I just saw Simon Watlington at the SNB with three Middle Eastern guys doing what looked like business, right before I met you for lunch."

"Did he see you?"

Ross shook his head. "I don't think so."

The elevator doors hissed open, and they walked to room one twenty-six.

"Maybe Mister Watlington just has a bank account there, and that's it. Maybe those three guys were students in his class," said Lin.

"Yeah, maybe," said Ross doubtfully.

Ross slipped the electronic coded plastic keycard into its slot.

The small door lock light turned from red to green.

Click.

The door unlocked and Ross held it open.

Lin went inside the room first.

Ross entered the threshold but automatically turned his back to close and lock the door.

Then all hell broke loose.

Lin was no more than five steps inside when someone grabbed her by the right arm, violently swinging her around and slamming her into the wall.

Lin collapsed unconscious to the floor. Ross immediately spun around to find an intruder standing in the middle of the room.

It was one of the men Ross had seen in the bank chatting with Watlington.

The man was in his late twenties with a medium build, and three or four inches shorter than Ross. He had a dusky complexion with short cropped oily black hair, and a small black moustache with three or four days' worth of facial whiskers. The man was wearing a pinstriped light blue suit with a white open collared shirt. In his right hand he was holding a Russian Makarov pistol. The pistol had a suppressor threaded onto the barrel to muffle the noise of any shots.

The primal instinct in Ross's subconscious instantaneously took over.

Attack.

Ross lunged at the intruder.

He grabbed the man's pistol hand with both of his, trying to wrestle the weapon free.

Ross applied pressure, and viciously twisted the man's fingers backwards.

Snap!

Snap!

Two of the man's fingers broke, allowing the Makarov pistol to drop harmlessly onto the carpeted floor.

Ross released the gunman's hand and went for this throat.

The intruder fell over backwards taking Ross on top of him, crashing to the floor.

With the intruder squirming desperately beneath him, Ross brought the palm of his right hand to the shocked assassin's chin and savagely snapped the man's head to the left and downward to the floor, breaking his neck.

The intruder stopped struggling. His eyes became fixed and stared off into the black void.

The assassin was dead.

Ross picked up the Makarov pistol. He realized it was too long to conceal the way it was, so he unscrewed the suppressor from the pistol barrel. Then he put the suppressor in his one suit coat pocket and the pistol in the other.

Ross took a deep breath in through his nostrils and slowly let it out between his pursed lips.

He pushed himself up off the floor and went over to Lin.

Lin was already coming around.

Ross knelt down by her side and gently shook her by her shoulders.

"Lin, are you all right?" asked Ross.

Lin sat up on the floor and shook the cobwebs out of her head. She drew in a shaky breath.

"Yes, yes. My God, what happened?"

She shook her head again to clear the spots that were creeping across her vision.

Then Lin saw the body on the floor.

"Who is that?"

Ross said, "I saw him with Watlington at the bank this morning."

"What? Oh my God. Is he dead?" asked Lin.

Ross stood up and went back over to the corpse.

He knelt down on one knee and checked the man's carotid pulse.

"Yes," said Ross, matter-of-factly.

Ross frisked the body, searching for a wallet or any other papers the man may have been carrying.

He pulled a passport out of the inner pocket of the man's suit coat, and a wallet out of his back trousers pocket.

Ross stood up.

He opened the passport and flipped through the pages.

It was a Pakistani passport issued to Mullah Akhtar Tayyab.

The photo inside was an exact likeness of the dead man's face.

"Judging by the amount of entry and exit stampings in this passport, Mister Tayyab was one well-traveled fellow," said Ross.

"It looks like he's recently been to Afghanistan, Libya, Mali, and Egypt."

Ross opened the wallet and found some interesting items.

Inside was three thousand Swiss Francs in cash, an international driver license issued to Mister Tayyab, various phone numbers and addresses on a small folded piece of paper, and the business card of a professor at the University of Zurich.

It was the business card of Professor Simon Watlington.

Ross pocketed the passport and wallet.

He turned to Lin and helped her stand up.

"Lin, things are really going to heat up now. Watlington is the terrorist financier for sure."

Lin was startled and confused.

"But how? How could it be so?"

Ross pointed to the dead man.

"Lin, that body is proof enough."

"What are we going to do?" asked Lin, clearly shaken.

Ross thought for a moment.

"We can assume that Watlington knew about my presence in the bank. That's why old Mullah here came over."

"I can't go to the embassy about this. Watlington is one of their own. The folks at State just simply wouldn't believe me."

Lin recalled back to her time working at the US Embassy in Kuala Lumpur.

"That's true, and the only other friend we have here is Emanuel," offered Lin.

"Yes," pondered Ross.

Ross pulled out his Blackberry and placed a call.

"Hello?" said a voice on the other end of Ross's cell phone.

"Emanuel?" said Ross into the Blackberry's mouthpiece.

"Yes?"

"This is Ross."

"Well hello Mister James. What can I do for you? Are you interested in a tour? I have three wonderful tours available that I can set up for you and Miss Lin at a very special rate."

Ross changed the substance of the conversation immediately.

"Emanuel, I need your assistance."

On the other end of the line, Emanuel could detect the urgency in his old friend's voice.

"Yes sir, what is it you need?"

"I'd like to interest you in a pest disposal job that requires use of your vehicle and certain insecticides," said Ross.

Emanuel was silent for a few seconds.

"I see. How big is the pest problem, sir?"

Ross said, "At least three more nests need to be thoroughly sprayed and cleaned out."

"I understand, sir."

"And I need a wheelchair too," added Ross.

"You need a wheelchair, sir?" Emanuel asked.

"Yes. An old friend of mine paid me a visit. He's taken ill now, and I'm afraid I need you to bring a wheelchair up to the room to help him outside."

Emanuel replied, "Ah, yes sir. I believe I can fix you right up, sir."

"And Emanuel, bring some extra blankets with the wheelchair. It's pretty cold outside."

"Yes, extra blankets, of course. Yes sir."

"I'll get the insecticides, wheelchair, and blankets immediately, sir. I assume time is of the essence here, right sir?"

"Yes, yes it is," said Ross.

"Very well Mister James. I'll need to stop over at my cousin's restaurant to get the supplies. They've had rodent problems before. Give me about an hour, sir."

"Thanks Emanuel," said Ross.

"You're very welcome, sir."

Ross pressed the end call button on his Blackberry cell phone and hung up.

"Okay. Emanuel is going to help. He'll be here in an hour."

Ross walked over to the room's front door and opened it slightly. He leaned forward and stuck his head out, glancing quickly down each side of the hallway. Seeing no one, Ross pulled the "Do Not Disturb" placard from the rear of the door, and placed it into the entry key slot on the front. He carefully closed the door and locked it with the deadbolt.

CHAPTER ELEVEN

STENCH OF DEATH

Bringgg!

Bringggg!

Bringggggg!

Ross picked up the receiver of his room's courtesy desk telephone.

"Hello?"

"Yes sir, it's me. I'm here. I've got the chair."

It was Emanuel.

"Okay, I'll be right down."

He placed the receiver back in its cradle, and looked at Lin.

"Emanuel is here. I'm going down to help with the wheelchair. I'll be back in a few."

"Okay Jamie. Be careful."

Lin always called Ross by that name when she was worried…or frightened.

Ross took the elevator down to the lobby.

He saw a man wearing an oversized gray US Air Force parka sitting in one of the chairs next to the receptionist's desk.

Next to him was a wheelchair.

Good old Emanuel.

Emanuel immediately stood up.

"Hello sir. I've got the chair you need right here."

"Thanks Emanuel. Let's get it upstairs."

The lovely gothic-styled receptionist, Saskia, was watching Ross and Emanuel.

"May I assist you gentleman?" she asked.

Ross turned to Saskia and smiled.

"My friend upstairs is feeling ill. Mister Mesiyas was kind enough to bring this wheelchair over for him."

"Is it anything serious, sir?"

Ross shook his head.

"No, I don't think so. It's probably the flu, but he's feeling a little weak so we have this chair for him. I'll feel better once I get him home in his bed."

"I see sir. Well, let me know if you need any help," said Saskia.

"Thank you, but I'm sure we can manage. Thanks again."

Saskia flashed her marvelous smile.

Ross and Emanuel rode in the elevator up to the third floor.

"Mister James?"

"Yeah?"

"Pardon me for asking, but is the problem up in your room the same kind of problem you had in Manila?"

Ross stared straight ahead at the elevator doors.

"Yes. Yes it is."

Emanuel said, "I see. Well, how many people are on your side in this?"

Ross turned his head and looked directly into Emanuel's eyes. He held up two fingers, indicating Lin and himself.

Emanuel looked at Ross's gesture and thought for a moment. Then Emanuel held up three fingers, showing he was with them.

Once they exited the elevator, Emanuel pushed the wheelchair behind Ross down the plush red carpeted hallway to room one-two-six.

Ross knocked three times.

"Who is it?" asked Lin behind the door.

"It's me, James."

Lin retracted the deadbolt and turned the lock hasp to the left. She opened the door, allowing Ross with Emanuel pushing the wheelchair to enter, and then immediately locked it.

"Okay, let's get started," said Ross.

Ross walked over to the body of Mullah Akhtar Tayyab.

Emanuel eased the wheelchair over and positioned it directly beside the body. He took the blankets off the seat and dropped them to the floor.

Ross positioned himself at the shoulders and Emanuel took the feet.

Together, both men lifted the corpse of the assassin and placed him sitting upright in the chair.

Emanuel picked up one blanket and used it to tuck in the body. He draped the other blanket around the shoulders and hooded the head of the corpse, allowing just enough of the face to be seen so as not to look suspicious.

"How's that, sir?"

Ross stared at the Pakistani assassin who tried to kill him a little more than an hour ago.

"He looks fine."

Ross turned to Lin.

"We all need to get out of here and now. This guy's friends will get pretty suspicious when he doesn't report back."

Ross looked into Emanuel's eyes.

"Where can we get rid of this?"

Emanuel already had thought about it on the way over and had formulated a plan.

"The, um, incinerator used by my cousin, sir. It's right behind her restaurant. That's the best bet."

"Fine," said Ross.

Ross pulled out the three thousand Swiss Francs that the assassin had been carrying and gave it to Emanuel.

"Here, take this."

Emanuel took the wad of cash and shoved it into the right front pocket of his faded blue jeans.

"Let's go," said Ross.

Emanuel spoke up again.

"Ah, Mister James, it really is pretty chilly out there. You and Miss Lin may want to bundle up."

Ross went to his suitcase and pulled out the fur lining for his trench coat. He zipped it in and put on the garment as Lin threw her tan winter overcoat onto her shoulders.

"Come on," said Ross.

With Emanuel handling the wheelchair, all three friends left the room and rode the elevator down to the lobby of the Hotel Bristol.

As they rolled past the front desk, Saskia said, "I hope your friend starts feeling better soon, sir."

"I'm sure he will, thank you," said Ross.

It was twenty-eight degrees Fahrenheit outside and snow was playfully floating down again blanketing everything in sight.

Emanuel had his taxi parked in front of the hotel in a handicapped spot. He maneuvered the wheelchair to where it was just behind and to the side of the right rear passenger door. Then he applied the brakes on the wheelchair and pulled out his car keys. He opened the right rear passenger door and assisted Ross in carefully lifting the body of Mullah Akhtar Tayyab out of the wheelchair. They placed him sitting upright innocently in the backseat with his seat belt securely fastened.

The Ford Mondeo was parked directly across the strasse, facing the opposite direction. Ross pulled the keys out of his pocket and handed them to Lin. His breath was coming out in condensed puffs, circling and disappearing skyward as he leaned over and gently kissed Lin on the cheek.

"Okay Lin, I'll ride with Emanuel and you follow us in my car."

"Right," replied Lin.

Ross waited for Lin to cross the strasse before he got into the left rear passenger seat of Emanuel's taxi. He buckled himself in and turned around to look out the back window.

Emanuel was back there, folding up the wheelchair and placing it into the trunk. He slammed the trunk lid down.

Thump.

Then Emanuel shuffled around to the drivers' side and opened the door.

"So far so good, sir," said Emanuel, huffing and puffing as he sat down.

Ross remained silent.

Emanuel slid the Mercedes key into the ignition switch and turned it sharply to the right. The V-8 engine sputtered with a few coughs and then roared to life.

He glanced into the rear and side view mirrors only once. Then Emanuel engaged the stick shift and expertly steered the 1972 Mercedes-Benz S-Class away from the curb and out into the traffic flow on Stampfenbachstrasse.

The 6.9 liter V-8 engine was having no issues churning through the wintry sludge, and Ross grew to appreciate the self-leveling heavy duty suspension.

Emanuel had programmed his GPS system to navigate directly to his cousin's restaurant.

"How long before we get there?" asked Ross.

"Oh, in this snow, about twenty-five minutes, sir."

Emanuel looked in the rearview mirror and verified that Lin was following them.

“I really appreciate your help in this, Emanuel,” said Ross.

“Think nothing of it, sir.”

Ross pulled out the wallet of the dead terrorist. He extracted and unfolded the piece of paper with the phone numbers and addresses.

“Emanuel, there are four addresses here on this piece of paper I found on our friend,” said Ross, motioning to the scrap of paper, “complete with phone numbers.”

“Three of them I recognize as Swiss National Bank locations in Basel, Geneva, and Zurich.”

Ross held up the piece of paper.

“But this fourth number and address is curious. I’m going to plug this into my cell phone GPS and see what comes up.”

Emanuel continued looking forward through the windshield at the traffic.

“Good idea, sir.”

Ross took out his cell phone and inputted the address into the GPS feature.

The display popped up showing the directions to whatever was at Talstrasse number six-five-four.

Emanuel started to slow down.

“There’s the restaurant, sir.”

Ross looked out his side window.

There across the street was a modern looking restaurant with an overhead sign proclaiming *Asiatisches Essen* in German.

“That’s your cousin’s restaurant?” asked Ross.

“Yes sir. That’s Lailani and Lars’ restaurant, specializing in Philippine cuisine.”

"The sign means *Asian Food* in English," proudly explained Emanuel.

"Oh," smiled Ross.

Emanuel took a sharp turn left and drove behind the restaurant.

"There it is, sir," said Emanuel.

In front of them was a cinderblock building with a corrugated steel roof and a large roll-up garage door front entrance.

Emanuel parked in front of the building. Lin had been following close and pulled up behind Emanuel.

"Excuse me, sir."

Emanuel got out of the car and walked back to Lin. She was already lowering the window.

"Miss Lin," said Emanuel, "I think it best if you please remain in the car until we get done with this. It won't take very long."

"I will," she said, looking nervous.

Emanuel walked back to his taxi and pressed the trunk button on his keychain.

Wump.

The trunk popped open and Emanuel reached in to retrieve the wheelchair.

Ross got out and opened the right rear passenger door. He started to shift the body to the edge of the seat.

Emanuel brought the wheelchair around as close as he could. He assisted Ross in lifting the corpse up and placing it into the chair.

This time Ross pushed the wheelchair through the snow and followed Emanuel around to the right side of the building.

There he witnessed Emanuel trying to open a single steel door with a key.

Emanuel could easily insert the key and turn it to the left, but the door wouldn't budge.

"God," exclaimed Emanuel, "this thing is frozen shut!"

"Here, let me help," said Ross.

Together, both men pushed against the door with their shoulders. Still it wouldn't open.

Ross said, "Okay, one more time as a team. On the count of three."

"Ready?" asked Ross.

"Ready," answered Emanuel.

"One …"

"… two …"

"… three!"

Both men slammed their shoulders against the steel door simultaneously.

Crrrunch!

The ice shattered with hundreds of tiny flakes showering their faces.

One more shove and the door opened.

Ross pushed the wheelchair inside. Emanuel flipped on the lights and quickly walked over to the incinerator.

The two front doors of the incinerator were cast iron and semi-circular on top. Each door had the date "28 July 1918" stamped on its face.

The incinerator's walls were eighteen inches thick all around, constructed from red fire brick with heavy tie rods. The walls ran all the way up and through the ceiling to form an outside exhaust shaft.

Emanuel picked up a crowbar and pried open the front doors.

Emanuel's cousin always kept the incinerator lit and working, out of concern that freezing would occur if it was left inactive.

The anticipated blast of heat was a welcome relief from the freezing temperatures outside.

The inside of the incinerator could easily accommodate large boxes of kitchen trash, tree limbs, or as in this case, more than enough room for the dead body of a terrorist.

Not wasting any time, Ross got the body around the shoulders and Emanuel grabbed the legs.

With one thrust, Ross and Emanuel heaved the body in head first.

Jesus Christ, thought Ross.

I feel like a God damn Nazi burning Jews in the death camps.

Mullah Akhtar Tayyab's corpse began to sizzle and pop from the intense flames.

Within seconds, the putrid smell of burning flesh permeated the air.

Christ, thought Ross.

He had smelled death before in the Philippines, Iraq, and Afghanistan.

Death was something Ross had experienced throughout his military career.

Death had a peculiar stench he could never get used to.

Emanuel picked up the crowbar and used it to swing the doors closed.

“Well that’s it, sir. Don’t worry, it’s just like he was cremated, that’s all.”

Ross said flatly, “He was a terrorist and assassin. He tried to kill us in the hotel room.”

Emanuel’s expression turned into a scowl.

“Maybe we should have thrown him into the river to give the fish something to eat.”

Both men turned around and walked towards the building exit, intent on allowing the incinerator to accomplish its work. Once outside, Emanuel pulled shut the side door and locked it.

“Well sir, that’s that. Might I suggest that Miss Lin remain here at the restaurant with my cousin?”

“That’s a good idea,” said Ross, “but you’re going to remain here as well. You’ve done enough for me already.”

“Ah, we’ll talk about that later, sir. Come on, I’ll introduce you to my relatives.”

CHAPTER TWELVE

JIHAD

Emanuel discovered the restaurant was closed.

He phoned his cousin and found out they were all over at their daughter's high school play. It was a production of *Les Misérables*. A flat tire was causing them to be delayed in returning home. Emanuel explained the circumstances to Lin and Ross.

"Time, and possibly existence as we know it stops, when you have a flat tire. Flat tires occur throughout a person's life. The better equipped and knowledgeable you are to handle them, the smoother your ride will be on the autobahn of life."

Lin smiled, and Ross just gave up trying to figure out what the hell Emanuel had just said.

Emanuel had his own keys to the establishment. His cousin Lailani had provided them in case he needed to come in for a warm cup of coffee during the odd hours he kept as a taxicab driver.

Emanuel unlocked the place and led Ross and Lin into the kitchen.

"Lailani says it's okay if Miss Lin hangs out here for a while. Take off your coats and have a seat. I'll make some coffee."

Emanuel removed his parka and threw it over a chair. Ross noticed a coat rack in the kitchen. He helped Lin out of her jacket and hung it up. Then he peeled off his trench coat and shook the snow off it before hanging it next to Lin's coat.

They sat down on stools behind a stainless steel kitchen counter while Emanuel busied himself putting on the coffee.

Ross took the opportunity to explain the situation to Lin.

"Lin, the same man I saw with Watlington in the bank just tried to kill us. I know that Watlington sent him. There's no doubt about it. And when he doesn't report back, Watlington will send more killers. So, I've got to get to him first."

Emanuel walked over and placed two steaming cups of coffee down in front of them.

"Here you go," said Emanuel. "Anyone need cream or sugar?"

Lin asked, "Do you have Sweet'n Low?"

"You mean the stuff in the pink packets?"

"Yes."

Emanuel scratched his head.

"I think so. I'll find some for you."

Emanuel scuttled off in search of the low calorie artificial sweetener.

Ross explained, "Lin, I've got one lead to follow. It's an address on Talstrasse."

"But what's there?" asked Lin.

"I don't know," Ross paused, "but I've got to find out."

Emanuel returned with the sweetener and spoke up.

"I seem to recall Talstrasse as being a warehouse district. I took a client there a while ago who had a storehouse full of Chinese imports. It's about a thirty minute ride."

Lin asked, "Why? Why do you have to do this? Why can't you call the police?"

"Because they would never believe me. And while they were trying to sort things out, Watlington would run," said Ross. "And I just can't allow that. I can't allow him to continue funding terrorism against the United States."

While the three friends were talking inside the Asiatisches Essen restaurant, the winter wonderland outside was being quietly disturbed.

Three cars pulled in from off the strasse.

The cars circled and probed the restaurant front parking lot.

They were German Audi vehicles.

Two were Audi A8 sedans, and one was an Audi Q5 sport utility vehicle.

All three were enameled in brilliant black metallic paint.

The snow crunched under the constant turning of the tires.

The scene was reminiscent of three cockroaches scurrying across a crisp white linen bed sheet.

Silhouettes of people could be seen inside the vehicles.

Several of the silhouettes seemed to be conversing on cell phones or some type of communications equipment.

After several seconds, the reconnaissance halted.

The three cars pulled over and parked professionally side by side.

Doors opened, and several men got out of each vehicle.

All the men were well dressed in dark overcoats and suits.

They appeared to be of Middle Eastern descent.

A team of two men walked forward and deliberately placed a small military-style backpack about five meters from the front door of the restaurant. They leaned over and began adjusting something on the top of this rucksack. Inside that pack was a brushed stainless steel, six quart, self locking lid, light-emitting diode display, common pressure cooker. The pressure cooker had been converted into an improvised explosive device.

Another team of two men split up and walked over to each of the far sides of the restaurant, one to the left and one to the right.

These men simultaneously lit the wicks protruding from the Molotov cocktails in their hands.

Inside the restaurant, Lin immediately became troubled.

The coffee cup she was holding dropped from her fingers and shattered to pieces on the tile floor.

She started trembling and shaking.

Lin closed her eyes and opened her subconscious mind.

She knew they were in danger.

Evil was in their presence.

Death was walking right through the front door.

Instantaneously her eyes opened wide.

"Get down quick!" yelled Lin.

Just then two Molotov cocktails came crashing through the front windows.

Lin reached out and pushed Emanuel over and off his feet. He fell backwards to the floor first.

Then Lin flung herself on top of Ross and pulled him to the floor with her.

The incendiary devices, commonly referred to as Molotov cocktails, were wine bottles filled with gasoline and motor oil. The wicks protruding from their cork stoppers were made of cloth.

These homemade firebombs shattered as they broke through the windows and ignited, creating a burning inferno inside the restaurant.

KA-BOOOM!

The pressure cooker bomb inside the knapsack went off, blowing the front door to smithereens.

Hundreds of red hot steel ball bearings shot into the restaurant, paving a path of destruction in their wake.

The only reason that Ross, Lin, and Emanuel weren't shredded to pieces was the quick thinking of Lin, and the stainless steel kitchen counter they were behind.

The inside of the restaurant became a sea of flames as the added motor oil caused the burning gasoline to stick everywhere.

Lin wrapped one of her arms around Ross's waist, and the other around Emanuel's waist. Ross and Emanuel put their arms around her shoulders.

Using her strength and body mass to support both of the semiconscious men, Lin led them through the backdoor and outside.

She shuffled Ross and Emanuel over to the Ford Mondeo and propped them against it. Both men were gasping and trying to cough the smoke out of their lungs.

The interior of the restaurant was now a complete holocaust.

Dining tables and chairs caught fire like matchsticks, along with the alcohol, linen, and draperies. The fire rapidly crawled from the walls to the ceiling. Waves of scorching heat were partnered with plumes of billowing smoke that were swallowing the building. The entire restaurant was totally engulfed and being consumed by the flames.

Lin fumbled with the car keys.

She hastily pressed the button and engaged the automatic door opener.

Ross and Emanuel were coming around now as Lin shoved them both into the backseats of the Mondeo.

She hurried around to the drivers' side and threw herself behind the steering wheel.

Lin had never started a car faster in her life as she jammed the key into the ignition switch and ratcheted it to the right.

The engine immediately came on, as well as a multitude of blue illuminated gauge lights.

Lin pushed the black button on the automatic shifter and slammed the transmission into drive.

The Ford Mondeo churned through the snow and ice as the V-6 263 horsepower engine proved its worth.

The seventeen inch aluminum wheels with Dunlop Winter Sport tires sliced through the sleet and sludge like snow boots with crampons, as the car tore around the corner and sped towards the front parking lot.

The al-Qaeda terrorists were shocked to see the Mondeo roaring around the corner and charging at them with Lin behind the wheel.

Wadoud Fahd Saeed reached inside his suit coat and pulled out his Makarov 9x18 millimeter pistol.

Saeed was hardcore al-Qaeda and was not going to let an infidel woman get past him.

He assumed the classic shooter's stance and leveled the pistol at the face behind the windshield of the onrushing automobile.

"Allahu Akbar!" yelled Saeed.

Those were the last words that ever came out of his mouth.

Lin pressed the gas pedal to the floor and slammed the Mondeo into the man.

Saeed's body crumpled like paper as Lin accelerated and completely ran him over with the two hundred and sixty-three galloping horses under the Ford's hood.

The al-Qaeda assassins were caught off guard as they saw Saeed get smashed like a grape in a wine press.

Abubakar Ali al-Shallah was contemplating whether to shoot his pistol or run to his car.

He decided to run to his car.

It was the last decision he ever had to make.

Al-Shallah turned to run, but slipped on the ice and fell down hard on his buttocks.

Lin ran over him.

The car rocked violently up and down as the man's body passed underneath its wheels. Lin took a quick glance back and saw the snow turn crimson. Her car broke the assassin's back, and ground him into the icy pavement like you would grind coffee beans.

The rest of the al-Qaeda terrorists saw what had happened and scrambled to their cars.

Ross and Emanuel had now recovered in the backseats of the Mondeo. Ross slid himself legs first over and into the left front passenger seat next to Lin.

The Ford Mondeo raced out from the parking lot and into the street.

Lin didn't know where she was going.

She only knew that she had to get away from these killers as fast as she could.

The Mondeo charged down the street with Lin desperately seeking an escape route.

Ross saw a green and white sign up ahead for the autobahn.

He quickly pointed to the placard.

"Take that exit!"

Lin swerved the Mondeo dangerously to the right and just made the exit ahead of the abutments.

They were now accelerating rapidly down autobahn A3.

The A3 autobahn connects Zurich to the Swiss City of Basel, which is right on the border of Germany and France.

Unlike German autobahns, the autobahns in Switzerland have a top speed of one hundred and twenty kilometers per hour. That's about seventy-five miles per hour.

Lin was already doing ninety-five miles per hour.

Ross looked in the rearview mirror.

The three Audi's were behind them and gaining.

He noticed a wide-eyed Emanuel sitting upright in the backseat.

"How're you doing, Emanuel?" asked Ross.

"I'm good," Emanuel replied confidently. He reached into the left front pocket of his faded blue jeans and pulled out a pistol.

"Here you go sir. I brought this, but didn't have a chance to give it to you yet."

Emanuel tapped Ross on the shoulder with the handgun.

Ross reached back and took the weapon.

It was a Beretta model 71 pistol in .22 LR caliber.

"Where'd you get this?" asked a not-too-surprised Ross.

Ross pressed the release button and pulled the magazine out. He verified that the Beretta was fully loaded with hollow point ammunition. Ross slid the magazine in and pulled the slide back, letting it snap forward to chamber a round. Then he engaged the weapon's safety lever.

"It's a long story sir, but a friend of mine worked for the Mossad in Tel Aviv and …"

"Okay, okay, I get it. Don't tell me anymore," said Ross, cutting him off.

Ross handed the Beretta back to Emanuel. "Here, keep it. I took a gun off the terrorist in the room."

The three Audi's were rapidly closing the distance to the Ford.

Lin was pushing hard on the 3.5 liter V-6 engine of the Mondeo.

"What can we do? Where can we go?" asked an impassioned Lin.

Before Ross could answer, one of the Audi A8's had pulled up to the left side of the Mondeo and matched their speed. Ross could clearly see the driver's face through the window. He turned his head in the other direction and could see the Audi Q5 SUV rapidly approaching on the right side.

"Lin, when I tell you to, I want you to floor it."

Lin could see the Audi on the left, and now she saw another one in her side mirror gaining on the right.

"Okay," said Lin.

Ross said, "On three."

"One …"

Ross brought the Makarov pistol up to his window and cocked back the hammer.

"… two …"

Ross held down the power button and lowered his passenger window.

"… three!"

Lin pressed the accelerator to the floor as Ross squeezed the Makarov's trigger twice.

KA-POW!

KA-POW!

The first bullet penetrated and shattered the driver's side window of the Audi A8. This bullet struck the driver in his right temple. The second bullet hit the man just above his right ear.

Blood and brains sprayed out the left side of the man's head and splattered across his windshield.

Lin gunned the Mondeo and raced forward doing over one hundred miles an hour.

The already dead man lost control of his car and veered to the right. At the same time, the terrorist driven SUV swerved left, as if to fill the void created when the Ford Mondeo surged forward.

The two Audi's struck each other and violently spun around in the middle of the autobahn.

An innocent driver in a passing Maserati couldn't get out of the way in time and slammed into the side of the Audi Q5, sending it smashing into its partner. The collision caused both terrorist vehicles to tumble over and burst into flames.

Emanuel turned around and saw the explosion on the autobahn.

"Two down, one to go," he said.

Lin was doing one hundred and five miles an hour presently, and the remaining terrorist car was rapidly overtaking them.

Ross looked over his right shoulder. The expression on the face of the terrorist behind the wheel of the black car was nothing short of maniacal rage. The assassin was hollering inside the car, hurling every obscenity known to man at the occupants of the fleeing vehicle.

Lin was pushing the Mondeo's screaming engine towards its limit at over one hundred and ten miles an hour now.

The Audi surged forward and rammed the rear end of the Mondeo.

KA-RUNK!

A viscerally frightened Lin gripped the steering wheel tighter. Her knuckles were turning white and her palms were getting sweaty despite the sub-freezing temperatures.

Emanuel hurriedly buckled his seat belt.

Ross knew it was only a matter of time…perhaps seconds…before the terrorists would start shooting at them.

KA-RUNK!

The Audi once again slammed into the rear of the Mondeo.

Ross saw that they were now whizzing by rows and rows of huge snow covered evergreen trees lining both sides of the autobahn.

A plan instantly formulated in Ross's mind.

"Lin, when I take hold of the steering wheel, just let go."

Lin looked perplexed.

"What? Umm, okay."

Ross gripped the steering wheel with his right hand.

He eased the Mondeo to the right, allowing just enough room for the Audi to slip on forward into the trap.

With a quick glance to the left, Ross saw the remaining Audi A8 was directly beside them. He could make out two men in the backseats. The right rear window was open, and one of the men had a Heckler & Koch MP5 nine millimeter submachine gun pointing directly at them.

Now!

Ross jerked the steering wheel to the left, which caused the Mondeo to slam into the right side of the Audi.

KA-RUNCH!

The impact sent the Audi careening wildly off the autobahn and into the tree line.

With gut wrenching screeching sounds of tearing metal, the Audi smashed head on into an enormous evergreen tree.

The steering wheel airbag deployed, but the impact was so great that the steering column dislodged and punctured the airbag and the driver's chest like a spear.

The two men in the backseats were equally unlucky.

They had not been wearing their seat belts.

Both of these men were sent flying forward and crashed headfirst through the windshield.

Their necks broke upon impact with the mammoth trunk of the evergreen tree.

Ross released the steering wheel back to Lin and said, "Try to pull over and park behind them."

Lin expertly took control of the Mondeo. She regained her composure and switched lanes. Finding the first available exit, Lin slowed down and pulled off the autobahn to the access road. She whipped the car around to the left, and backtracked to the scene of the collision.

Lin steered the Mondeo behind the Audi and parked. She left the engine running and looked at Ross.

"What now, James?" asked Lin.

"Wait here," said Ross.

Ross got out of the car.

With snowflakes floating down and Makarov in hand, Ross was freezing outside in his suit and tie as he briskly walked up to the drivers' side of the crashed Audi.

The impact had shaken loose an avalanche of snow from the limbs of the behemoth evergreen tree, and deposited it over the vehicle.

He peered inside where the windshield used to be.

The al-Qaeda driver was dead.

From the best that Ross could surmise, despite the airbag deployment, the hundred-mile-an-hour impact with the colossal evergreen tree trunk had pushed the steering column into the man's chest, puncturing and crushing it.

Ross searched the corpse and extracted his passport and wallet. He patted the body down and found the man was wearing a shoulder holster with handgun. It was a Sig Sauer P290 nine millimeter pistol. Ross pocketed the pistol and looked inside the vehicle for the MP5 submachine gun, but it was nowhere to be found.

Probably lying on the autobahn back there somewhere.

The dead terrorist had a Pakistani passport issued in the name of Rasool ur Ra'ahmah. Inside his wallet was an international driver license, a Visa platinum card, three tickets for the Wild Wadi Waterpark in Dubai, and banknotes in the sum of five thousand Swiss Francs.

He turned and looked at the twisted bodies of the other two terrorists. They were in a mangled heap between the impassive evergreen tree trunk and what was left of the Audi's front end.

Ross bent down and searched the bloody corpses.

No weapons.

All he could locate were their passports and wallets.

Ross stuck all of it into his suit coat pockets.

He walked back to the drivers' side. Leaning forward, Ross pulled the keys out of the ignition.

Emanuel had gotten out of the Mondeo and was standing behind the Audi, waiting to assist Ross. He was stomping his feet and rubbing his hands together trying to control his shivering.

Events at the Asiatisches Essen restaurant had transpired so quickly that Ross, Lin, and Emanuel hadn't the time to gather their outer winter garments.

Emanuel was freezing in his red flannel shirt and faded blue jeans. Lin was no better off in her spaghetti-strap knee-length red dress. She finally turned on the Mondeo's defrost and heater.

"Check the trunk," ordered Ross as he tossed the car keys over to Emanuel.

Emanuel pressed the button of the automatic opener.

Pah-rump!

The trunk popped open and Emanuel looked inside.

There was a medium sized black heavy duty reinforced nylon zipper bag, and a smaller olive drab colored cloth satchel with shoulder strap.

Ross glanced back and saw that Lin was sitting inside the Mondeo trying to stay warm. He walked over to Emanuel.

Ross looked at Emanuel and nodded his head.

"Let's see what's in those," Ross said.

With shaking, trembling fingers, Emanuel unzipped the black nylon bag. He spread the mouth of the bag open and peered inside with Ross.

Something was glittering back up at them.

Inside the nylon bag rested three gold bars.

"Wow," said a surprised Emanuel. "That there's gold, sir."

Ross reached in with numb fingers and picked up one of the bars.

It was more like a brick, only heavier.

Very much heavier.

"This has to weigh twenty-five pounds at least," remarked Ross.

"Well oh my goodness," said an astonished Emanuel.

On the face of the gold bar were proof marks from the 1943 Berlin Reichsbank.

It also had the stampings of the Nazi eagle perched on top of a wreathed Swastika.

"How much do you think one of these is worth?" asked Emanuel.

Ross thought a moment.

"The value of gold fluctuates daily with the market. Some days it's up, and some days it's down. I believe gold is currently valued at around fourteen hundred American dollars per ounce, give or take."

Emanuel picked up a gold bar and hefted it in his hands.

Ross pulled out his smartphone and scrolled to the calculator function.

"So, if one of these bars weighs twenty-five pounds, and there are sixteen ounces in a pound, that would be …"

Ross punched in the numbers.

"That would mean this bar is worth …"

Emanuel waited with literally frozen breath.

"What? What is it worth?" anxiously asked Emanuel.

Ross stared at the figure from the calculator.

"That would mean this one gold bar is worth five hundred and sixty thousand dollars, American."

Emanuel stared at the gold in his hand.

"Are you serious, sir?"

"Yep. You're holding half a million dollars in your hands, Emanuel," said Ross.

No man uttered a word for several seconds.

Ross replaced the gold bar he was holding back into the nylon bag. He reached over and flipped up the cover flap of the smaller olive drab colored cloth satchel.

Inside were military explosives.

The satchel contained four sheets of M118 PETN.

Pentaerythriol Tetranitrate, known by its abbreviation as PETN, is a plastic explosive that comes in thin, half pound sheets. It is a flexible explosive with pressure sensitive adhesive tape on one side to attach to whatever you want to destroy. PETN was designed as a cutting charge for steel targets. It's known for having high shattering and fragmentation characteristics.

Also in the satchel were blasting caps, wires, and electronic detonator timing devices.

"Everything the well-dressed anarchist needs," said Emanuel.

Ross picked up the explosives satchel by its strap and slung it over his right shoulder.

"Let's get this stuff in the car."

The reinforced black nylon bag weighed at least seventy-five pounds from the three gold bars. Ross went to grab it, but Emanuel stopped him.

"Here sir, let me do that."

Emanuel grabbed the nylon bag by its handle straps and hoisted it up and out of the trunk of the Audi. He shuffled over to the Mondeo with the sagging bag of gold.

Ross walked ahead of him and motioned for Lin to roll down her window.

Luxurious waves of heat cascaded from the open window.

"Pop the trunk," said Ross.

Emanuel waited and then plopped the gold bag into the trunk, and slammed the lid shut.

"Sir, perhaps I should relieve Miss Lin and take over the driving now?"

Lin overheard the conversation and said, "I think that's a good idea."

Lin got into the rear of the Mondeo while Ross sat up front next to Emanuel. They all buckled their seat belts.

Emanuel pulled the car out onto the autobahn and headed south.

He shortly had the Mondeo purring at the posted autobahn speed of one hundred and twenty kilometers per hour.

Ross reached back and handed the Sig Sauer P290 pistol to Lin.

"Here, take this."

Lin took the pistol and held it loosely on her lap.

"I found that on the driver of the Audi," explained Ross.

Emanuel kept his hands on the steering wheel and looked straight ahead. He thought about the bag of explosives around the shoulder of his friend, and his girlfriend in the backseat.

"What's the plan, sir?"

Ross pulled out his smartphone and powered up the Global Positioning System.

"I take it we're going to number six-five-four Talstrasse?" asked Emanuel.

"Yeah," said Ross, "it's all we've got left."

Ross scrolled through the addresses on the GPS.

“We’ve been targeted at the hotel.”

Ross found the address and pressed the “GO!” button.

“We were followed and targeted at the restaurant.”

Ross adjusted the GPS volume control higher.

“There’s no reason to go to the banks since we have all the proof we need right in the trunk.”

“Proof of what?” asked Lin.

Ross stared out his side window at the innocent snowflakes falling gently and playfully over the countryside.

“Proof of what?” asked Lin again.

Ross said, “Proof that our friend, the Honorable Simon Watlington, is a terrorist financier.”

CHAPTER THIRTEEN

OUT OF TIME

Talstrasse road runs south through Zurich. At the end, you will find the Burkliplatz Square with its bus and tram stations. A little further on, you will see the lakeshore quay and the harbors with their piers filled with boats to ferry you across Lake Zurich. From the waterfront to the square is the Talstrasse warehouse district.

Talstrasse 654 was right in the heart of the Altstadt, or Old Town historical area.

The weather had gotten worse with blustery winds and drifts of snow. It was dusk by the time they arrived at their location.

Emanuel parked the Mondeo across the street, and left the engine running.

"There it is sir, number six-five-four Talstrasse. Looks just like all the other warehouses around here."

Ross was silent. He was visually casing the area for any activity. Then he noticed the cameras.

There were two surveillance cameras perched on the far right and left eaves of the building.

"They've got surveillance up there on the roof," said Ross, "so we can assume they've already seen us."

"Pull around to the rear," instructed Ross.

Emanuel slowly drove the snow-laden Ford Mondeo to the back.

There they found what appeared to be a community parking lot filled with service trucks and privately owned vehicles.

Ross spotted the soot covered hulk of a Mercedes-Benz delivery truck.

"Park next to the Benz truck."

Emanuel nodded and maneuvered the Mondeo to the right side of the truck.

He shifted the Ford into park and kept the motor running with the heat on. Then he sat back and looked at Ross.

"So what's the plan, boss?" asked Emanuel.

No sooner had Emanuel mouthed the words, than the plan was ultimately revealed.

High intensity floodlights suddenly flashed on, illuminating the entire parking lot.

Ross looked around.

"Those could have turned on because they're preset for nighttime, or …"

Lin filled in the sentence.

"Or because they know we're here and they're watching us."

"Exactly," said Ross.

As if to quantify the answer, a security light immediately flickered on above the rear door of the warehouse.

The three of them watched with curiosity as the rear door opened, and there stood the imposing six foot four inch tall figure of Simon Watlington.

Watlington was immaculately attired in a three piece gray suit.

There was a cigarette perched between his lips.

He slid his hand in his suit coat and extracted a cigarette lighter. Popping open the top of the lighter, he flicked the thumbwheel downward. The welcome spark ignited a wavering blue flame.

Holding the lighter flame to the cigarette between his lips, Watlington cocked his head to the side and allowed himself the luxury of a long, slow draw.

He held the smoke in his lungs for a moment, and then snapped the little top back down on the lighter.

Tilting his head upwards, Watlington hissed the tobacco vapors out through his nostrils towards the descending snowflakes.

Glancing towards the parking lot, Watlington took another long, slow draw on his cigarette. Then with a flick of his fingers, Watlington sent what was left of his cigarette flying off like a tiny sputtering meteorite, drilling its way into the sludge of a nearby snow bank.

Taking one more glance skyward at the gently falling snow, Watlington now lowered his head while hunching up his shoulders, and walked back inside the warehouse. He left the rear door completely wide open.

Ross knew it was a proposition.

It was an open invitation for Ross, and no one else.

This was it.

This was how things would finally unfold.

Man to man.

Terrorist to soldier.

Ross knew there was no other way.

He reached inside his suit coat and pulled out a business card.

"Here Lin, take this."

Lin looked at Ross.

She looked at his rumpled black suit.

She looked at his thin black necktie highlighting his white shirt.

She looked at the handsome half Thai, half American face that she had grown to love.

She looked into his piercing dark brown eyes that she always could believe.

Lin reached forward and with her fingers brushed at the shock of brown hair that always fell across his forehead. It stayed put for a second, then just fell back down again.

"What's this?" asked Lin.

"It's the contact information for Lorrie Andrea. She's the Foreign Service Officer I met at the American Consular Agency." Ross reached into his pockets and pulled out all of the passports and wallets of the terrorists, and plopped them down on the backseat. "Give these to her."

"But …"

"They're on Dufourstrasse. Go there and notify her. Come back with as many armed security personnel as you can."

Lin looked at the card as tears formed in her eyes.

She knew what this was.

This was James Ross and his way of protecting her.

A single tear trickled down her cheek.

Emanuel saw Lin's face and quickly spoke up.

"Sir, I'll stay here and assist you."

"No," said Ross. "You go with Lin."

Emanuel said, "Wait a minute …"

Then Lin spoke defiantly.

"I'll go, only if you let Emanuel stay here and help you, and that's final."

Ross looked at Lin. He knew better than to argue further.

"Okay."

There was no time for sentimentality.

There was no time for goodbye kisses.

Ross looked once more at Lin in the backseat.

"Go quickly Lin," he said.

Ross turned to Emanuel.

"Come on."

Both men got out of the warmth of the car and were instantly blasted by the frigid temperatures.

Emanuel was shivering in his red flannel shirt and blue jeans, but at least his galoshes were keeping his feet warm and dry. He pulled the Beretta pistol out of his faded jeans pocket and held it at the ready.

Ross was faring no better in his suit. But at least he wasn't slipping too badly in his well-worn black leather shoes. He gripped the Makarov pistol in his right hand and held it inside the flap pocket of his suit coat like some mobster from a 1930s film.

Ross turned and saw that Lin was already driving out of the parking lot.

"Let's split up. I'll come in from the left side, you take the right, and I'll enter first," said Ross.

Emanuel nodded his head up and down affirmatively.

As he was walking forward, Ross was scanning the windows of the warehouse for activity. He was looking for possible snipers.

Emanuel did the same as he cautiously crept forward through the snow and reached the right side of the door frame.

Ross reached his position and pulled out his pistol.

"On three," Ross whispered.

Emanuel gave a thumbs' up acknowledgement.

"One …"

Emanuel cocked the hammer back on his Beretta.

"… two …"

Emanuel's shivering stopped.

"… three!"

Ross lunged through the open doorway with his pistol out in front.

He was about ten feet inside when something lightning fast slammed into the left side of his head and sent him tumbling over onto the concrete floor.

Emanuel was right behind Ross and ran to his aid.

But it was to no avail.

Emanuel was immediately walloped with a blinding sidekick that rocked his jaw and knocked him unconscious to the floor.

It was Watlington, the master of the Korean martial art of Hwa Rang Do.

Ross was near unconsciousness on the floor and having a hard time trying to get up.

Watlington grabbed Emanuel by his right wrist and savagely dragged him through the doorway, dislocating his shoulder in the process. He pulled Emanuel outside and dropped him in the snow. Then Watlington walked back inside and locked the door shut behind him.

Ross brought his knees up first, and then straightened his arms to push himself up. He staggered to his feet, pistol in hand, only to fall back down again.

He rolled over and agonizingly started the process again.

Reaching down using his knees as support, Ross wobbly straightened his legs and struggled to his feet.

He spat blood out of his mouth and shook his head to clear his blurred vision.

Ross still had a hold of his pistol as he faced his adversary.

"Now that your friend is gone, we can have a moment to ourselves," said Watlington.

For those who first encounter him, Simon Watlington can present a very imposing figure. At six feet four inches tall and weighing two hundred and twenty pounds, Watlington prided himself on staying in shape. His bald head was accented by thin, over-arching eyebrows that seemed to resemble quotation marks whenever he smiled. The left eyebrow had been cut in half decades ago by a scar he received from a fencing competition. His eyes were jade green in color, which caused people to stare at them unintentionally. His face was always clean shaven, with the smell of Obsession aftershave.

Ross had a hard time remembering that Watlington was a fifty-five year old man, after having just been almost knocked unconscious by him.

Watlington paced in front of Ross, fingering the gold Master Mason ring on the third finger of his left hand. He stopped pacing and looked at the Blancpain Fifty Fathoms chronograph on his left wrist, and smiled.

"We have time. I'm sure you sent Lin for the authorities. But we have time, all the time in the world actually."

"I have to give you credit, Captain Ross. I knew you were a remarkable man after I saw you in action in Kuala Lumpur. But this is …"

Watlington made a sweeping gesture with his right arm.

"This is simply unbelievable!"

"You arrived here just yesterday, and now see where we are!"

"Tell me, how did you get rid of my associates?"

Ross said, "You mean your assassins?"

Watlington nodded his head up and down in agreement.

"Ah yes, I know. They are the vermin of the street. They are no better than uncouth, vulgar animals."

Watlington was pacing and moving closer to Ross.

Ross held the Makarov pistol steady.

"That's quite close enough, sir," said Ross.

Watlington studied Ross.

"There's really no need for the gun, Captain Ross. I just want to talk."

Ross's facial expression was like a piece of iron.

"Like you just talked to Emanuel?"

Watlington acted surprised.

"Who? Oh, your taxi man? He does not factor into this equation whatsoever. He is merely a distraction here tonight. You should be pleased I did not kill him."

"Come on sir, let's go," said Ross, waving the pistol towards the exit.

"Go? Go where?" asked Watlington.

Ross replied, "I'm taking you to the cantonal police."

"Ha!" laughed Watlington. "You must be joking! Do you really think they will believe you?"

"I'm a respected member of the community!"

"I'm a university professor!"

Watlington smirked.

"But more importantly, I'm a faithful depositor to Swiss financial institutions!"

Watlington stopped pacing.

"No Captain Ross, it is I who am taking you."

"I think we can be mutually beneficial to each other."

"I need a man who is utterly reliable."

"I need a partner who is absolutely loyal."

"I need someone upon whom I can put my unreserved and complete trust."

Watlington thrust out his right arm and pointed his index finger at Ross.

"And that man is you, Captain Ross."

Ross shook his head from side to side in disagreement.

The words were crisp and clear, and the tone of the voice parleying them was cold and deadly.

"I'm a soldier, a soldier fighting terrorists. You fund terrorists, sir," said Ross. "Do the math."

Watlington frowned.

"My, my, my, Captain Ross. You are a stubborn man."

Watlington lowered his gaze and looked at the concrete floor of the warehouse for a few seconds, as if pondering what to do next.

"But it doesn't have to be like this."

"Stop and think, James."

"A friendship with me can be very financially lucrative for you and Lin."

Like Lucifer before him, Watlington let that piece of temptation sink in.

"But now, I'm going to show you something which I feel you will find truly fascinating."

"Before I do however, allow me to formally introduce myself."

Ross looked puzzled.

Watlington squared his shoulders and said, "I am the only surviving child of SS-Obersturmführer Wilhelm and Ingrid von Lugoff."

Ross slowly lowered his pistol as a look of astonishment crept across his face.

"I am Wolfram von Lugoff."

CHAPTER FOURTEEN

TIMELESS TERRORIST

Lugoff led Ross to the middle of the warehouse. There he pulled the tarpaulin off of a large thing.

"Captain Ross, this is it. This is a very special machine, a very special device."

The object was about the size of an automobile standing upright. It was about nine or ten feet wide, and fifteen feet tall. It was made out of some type of metal that Ross could not immediately identify. It appeared to be heavy, probably four to five thousand pounds. Its color was a faded dark metallic gray. It had crisscrossing electronic cables running around its base and up to its top. There appeared to be a hatch or door on what Ross could only guess was the front of the machine. Circling around the top of the machine appeared to be small windows or mirrors.

It very much resembled an old NASA Mercury capsule standing on end, or even a large metallic bell.

“Its military operational codename is *Die Glocke.*”

“What?” asked Ross.

“Translated from German into English, that literally means *The Bell,*” Lugoff explained.

“When the Third Reich was falling apart, my father, SS-Obersturmführer Wilhelm von Lugoff, was entrusted by his commander to safeguard Die Glocke.”

“Okay. Thanks for the history lesson,” said Ross. “Let’s go.”

Lugoff’s expression became deadly serious.

“Die Glocke is a machine that was created to stabilize fissionable materials for the Third Reich.”

“Oh,” said Ross.

“That was the official story anyway. But, my father was told that through operational testing, another use for Die Glocke was discovered.”

“What was that?” asked Ross.

“My father was told that Die Glocke could actually open a portal through time itself.”

“What?”

“Yes. It’s true. Die Glocke is a type of transporter to the past or the future. Through testing, Die Glocke was found to be able to transfer a man into the fourth dimension.”

“Uh-huh,” said Ross doubtfully.

“It is a time machine,” Lugoff revealed.

Ross kept the Makarov pistol leveled at Lugoff.

“My father believed that there could be enormous military implications for Die Glocke. They planned to transport select troops into the time vortex to conduct military operations that would guarantee total victory and win the war for the Fatherland."

"The engineer in charge of the V-2 missiles and Die Glocke was General Hans Kammler. It's even believed that his disappearance at the end of the war had something to do with this. Some said he transported himself to the future, and then returned the machine back to the present."

"Of course, I personally found all that hard to believe. But my father was very serious. So when I had the time I conducted my own research."

"I was determined to find out if what my father had told me of Die Glocke was accurate. If what my father said was true, Die Glocke in the proper hands could change the destiny of the world forever. The gold was always secondary."

Ross couldn't believe what he was hearing. He waved his pistol towards the warehouse exit and said, "Come on Watlington or Lugoff, whoever you are, let's go."

"Aren't you curious at all, Captain Ross? Don't you want to hear everything?"

Ross knew the more time he wasted in this warehouse, the better chance Lugoff would have confederates on the way.

But he had to admit the story was fascinating.

"Okay. Make it quick."

Lugoff looked pleased and continued his revelations.

"Upon his death, my father passed on to me the bank accounts. He designated me as the sole beneficiary. There are three of them, as you probably already know, since that's why you're here. One is in Basel, one in Geneva, and the one here in Zurich. They were filled with gold, Captain Ross…pilfered, World War Two, Third Reich gold."

"My father told me that the gold was worth twenty-eight million American, in 1944 dollars. He utilized the wealth to live on in Geneva after his escape from the Stasi. He bestowed the funds to finance my education and to give me a good life. It was more money than I could ever spend in one lifetime."

Lugoff studied Ross's confused expression.

"Ah, but you must be asking yourself how it came to all this."

"It did cross my mind," said Ross.

Lugoff smiled.

"Very few people in the world know that I am not really the Honorable Simon Watlington, former United States Ambassador to Malaysia. Over thirty years ago while on a State Department assignment in Berlin, Simon Watlington had been disfigured in a car wreck near Checkpoint Charlie."

"That was the official newspaper account anyway."

"The real Simon Watlington died in that accident. That car crash had been planned and prearranged years before. Simon Watlington had been chosen because he had no siblings, his father and mother were deceased, and he was a junior Foreign Service Officer whose career could be manipulated."

"The KGB had chosen and recruited me for that task."

"The automobile accident scenario had been planned and set up for years in advance by the KGB, intent on having a long-term controllable asset deep inside the United States government."

"The real Watlington's body had been switched in the counterfeit ambulance with me, the plastic-surgery-enhanced impostor. I had been covered in bandages and injuries, right down to the fictional facial and vocal cord burns. With the face permanently altered, and the distinct vocal cord changes, who would be the wiser? Any attempt at positive identification was physically impossible since the fingerprints had been burned off."

"Having assumed Watlington's identity, I rotated from position to position in the US State Department over the years."

"As the Bible says, I had become a wolf in sheep's clothing, Captain Ross. I was a sleeper agent unknown to all except my handlers, the KGB."

Lugoff studied Ross's face for a moment.

"I see you are puzzled," said Lugoff. "Bear with me."

"The Allies murdered my brothers and sister during the fire bombing campaign in Dresden. The Russians and their bastard East German Stasi stooges destroyed my father and mother. I vowed to extract my vengeance."

"I allowed the KGB to recruit me. I spent thirty-four years as a Foreign Service Officer. I rose to become the United States Ambassador to Malaysia, as you have seen. All the while, I was a KGB agent. For years I fed the Soviets secret information to slowly erode the security of the United States. I covertly financed al-Qaeda in the Middle East."

Ross was mesmerized.

"But why, why sell out the United States? Why finance terrorism against US soldiers? Why destroy America?" Ross asked incredulously.

"I'd have thought that would be obvious to you, Captain Ross."

"The Allies burned my brothers and sister to death!"

"Don't you understand?"

"The Third Reich would have been victorious if not for the entry of the United States into the war, that's why!"

"Anyone who was an enemy of the Reich and my father was an enemy to me!"

"I swore to my father to honor his birthright!"

Lugoff shifted his eyes and looked around the warehouse.

"Once I was sure I had secured the university position, I transferred everything from Geneva to here. My main base of operations became Zurich."

Lugoff clasped his hands behind his back and paced back and forth.

"I serve as a professor at the University of Zurich now, and I actually enjoy teaching that upper-level class on international terrorism."

He stopped pacing and stared at Ross.

"Young minds are so easily influenced and manipulated."

"But now Captain Ross, it's time for me to collect my due."

"Now it's time for them to pay *their* bill."

"I have been turning friend against friend, and foe against foe, for years."

"In the eighties, I secretly financed the Mujahedeen against the Russians."

"Little by little, I slowly eroded my parents' killers with a war."

"It was payback."

"It was a war as old as time."

"It was an asymmetrical war."

"It was a guerrilla war."

"It was classic unconventional warfare."

"And it will never cease."

"The Russians are fools. They try to control by brutal power. They had no idea of the forces I mounted against them."

Lugoff's eyes glazed over. He brought his elbows close to his sides and clenched his fists.

"Didn't they capture my father?"

"Didn't they torture him?"

"Didn't they defile my beloved mother?"

"Didn't they destroy my parents?"

"Those bastards!"

"I will never forget!"

"I will never forgive!"

"Now is the time!"

"Now is *my* time!"

Lugoff jabbed his right fist in the air and pointed his finger at Ross.

"Didn't I seek out their counsel?"

"Didn't I allow the Soviets to recruit me?"

Lugoff was yelling now.

"They thought they could control me!"

"They thought they could manipulate me out of fear!"

"See how easily they fell into my trap!"

"They emptied their barbaric filth on my family!"

Lugoff spread wide the fingers on his hands and brought his palms across his body in a wide crisscrossing throwaway gesture.

"Now, I have defied the entire world!"

Then Lugoff raised his right arm in the Hitler salute.

"I swear to this, just as surely as I am the son of SS-Obersturmführer Wilhelm von Lugoff!"

Ross was in uncharted territory now. He had never experienced anything even remotely resembling this.

This was maniacal.

This was insanity.

"Okay. Let's go, Wolfram. It's time to go now," cautiously said Ross, motioning with his pistol.

Lugoff laughed. "Do you really think I'm going to let you take me alive?"

Ross's expression became like stone. "Alive or dead, it doesn't much matter to me."

Two kilometers away, Lin arrived at Dufourstrasse 101. It was a nondescript, gray stone, four story governmental building.

She parked in front, and left the engine running with the heater and defroster turned on.

No sooner had she opened the car door than a blast of frigid air hit her causing her to catch her breath. She could feel her body vasoconstricting.

Lin shuddered for a second and then embraced the cold by sprinting up the front steps of the building.

Once inside, she raced down the hall to the bank of elevators.

Lin jammed her finger into the elevator “UP” button until it illuminated bright red and the twin elevator doors opened.

She rushed inside and punched the third floor button repeatedly. Anxiously waiting, Lin could hardly contain herself and was going over in her mind what to say, and how many security people she herself could carry in the Ford Mondeo.

The elevator doors hissed open and Lin ran out, searching up and down the hall for the offices of the American Consular Agency.

She found them.

The office was closed.

Their office hours were from ten o’clock in the morning until one o’clock in the afternoon, Monday through Friday.

The office had closed early today due to the current administration’s 2013 sequestration budget cutbacks.

“God damn it!” yelled Lin as she kicked the front door as hard as she could.

“God damn it!”

There came a sound from around the corner like a chair scrapping across the floor, and then suddenly a voice blurted out.

“They’re closed. Cutbacks you know. They won’t be open until tomorrow.”

Lin turned to see a blue uniformed Department of Defense contract security guard. He had been sleeping in his chair around the corner, and Lin’s ruckus woke him up.

The balding, fifty-eight year old, slightly overweight security guard sauntered over to Lin with an air of false bravado.

"They're closed, but I'm open babe," said the now cocky guard.

The man placed his hand on Lin's left shoulder.

"I'm here now, sweet thing."

Lin reacted on instinct. She reached down with her right hand and grabbed the man by his testicles.

Lin squeezed hard and twisted the man's family jewels sideways.

"Yeeeooowwww!"

The security guard let out a painful screech and then collapsed face first to the floor.

"I don't have time for nonsense," said Lin, matter-of-factly.

Back at the Talstrasse warehouse, Lugoff was continuing his diatribe.

"Captain Ross, don't be so naïve. You work for a government that would sell you out to Islamic radicals just for the sake of maintaining political correctness. Does Benghazi ring a bell?"

"Why, your own president is unwilling to even speak the words 'radical Islamic Jihadists.' He refuses to acknowledge and take into account their religious extremism."

"He's your president too," countered Ross.

"Indeed he is. But I can see the world for what it is. Do you really think the current administration cares about the greatness of the United States in the same way as JFK or Reagan did?"

"Hey, that's the US of A. you're talking about pal," quipped Ross.

"Ha!" laughed Lugoff. "Washington has been taken over by the new breed. They apologize for past glories. They think the masses will follow them if they just give them anything they want. Their disciples are low-information liberal fools who haven't the slightest idea of what it means to sacrifice for their country. They have created a culture of corruption. And, pray tell, how are you going to survive that? How are you, Captain James Ross, going to serve a master who loathes you?"

Ross kept quiet.

Lugoff answered his own questions. "You can't. He will destroy you, Captain Ross. But there is something you can do."

"What's that?" Ross spoke up.

Lugoff spread his arms wide.

"You can join me. You can become my ally. We can work together. No more will you have to squander your talents and serve fools. No more will you have to say 'yes sir' to leaders who should be relegated to shining your shoes."

Ross skeptically sighed deeply.

"And I'll make you rich. I can promise you wealth. You can finally marry Miss Sparrow and have the life you could only dare to dream about until now. *Esse quam videri,*" said Lugoff.

Ross knew the phrase.

"To be, rather than to seem to be," replied Ross. "That's from Aeschylus."

"Well, well, well, Captain Ross. You are an educated man. And all you have to do now is shake my hand."

Ross held the Makarov steady in his right hand. He slipped the satchel off his shoulders and over his head with his left hand.

Just then gunshots could be heard outside, and the rear door of the Talstrasse warehouse slammed open.

Silhouetted in the archway was Lin Sparrow, holding the Sig Sauer pistol. She had blasted apart the lock of the door.

"Jamie!" yelled Lin, "I've got Emanuel!"

Ross instinctively turned his head towards Lin.

Lugoff took advantage of the unexpected diversion.

He turned around and grabbed the handle on the entry hatch of Die Glocke.

With a wild counterclockwise spin and swift tug, the metal handle gave way and the hatch swung open.

Lugoff flung himself inside, clanging the door shut behind him.

Moving quickly, Lugoff spun the handle clockwise to secure himself in.

For a split second, Ross wondered what Lugoff and his degree in Applied Mathematics from the University of Geneva could make Die Glocke do.

He wondered if Lugoff had unlocked the secret of Die Glocke.

Take it to your grave, Lugoff, thought Ross.

In about three seconds he had his answer.

CHAPTER FIFTEEN

SOMEWHERE NEVER

There was a whirring sound coming from Die Glocke that was growing in intensity.

The base of the machine was emitting a greenish-orange glow, and the entire outer capsule was starting to vibrate.

Ross ran to Die Glocke and slid to his knees, dumping the explosives out of his satchel bag. He ripped the plastic coverings off of three sheets of M118 PETN to activate their adhesiveness. Quickly, he slapped the explosive sheets interlocking around the base of Die Glocke, creating a charge.

The PETN stuck like glue.

Then he ratcheted back the electronic detonator timer delay switch to thirty seconds, unfurled the bridge wire, and jammed the blasting cap into the charge.

Ross sprang to his feet.

“Run!” he yelled to Lin at the top of his lungs, while pointing to the exit.

Ross ripped off the plastic covering from a fourth sheet of PETN, exposing the adhesive backing. Then he stuck an electronic timing detonator to it, verified the bridge wire was connected, and pressed in the blasting cap. He quickly set the timer delay switch for twenty seconds.

Now he scrambled towards the exit.

On the way, Ross dropped this explosive charge into a huge metal bin full of floor dust particles and debris that was near the center of the warehouse.

He quickly caught up with Lin and grabbed her by the hand.

Together they made a wild dash for the warehouse exit.

Outside, the frigid Nordic air blasted into their lungs like a thousand sharp needles.

They ran about twenty meters and took refuge behind the soot covered hulk of the Mercedes-Benz truck.

“Get down!” yelled Ross.

Ross and Lin flopped facedown spread-eagled on the snow coated tarmac.

Lin covered her head with her hands.

Ross looked at his Benrus.

“Three …”

“… two …”

“… one …”

KA-BOOM!

The charge in the dust bin went off first, blowing up and out and electrifying the dust particles.

Two seconds later, the charge attached to Die Glocke ignited.

KA-BOOMMMMMM!

The blast tore into Die Glocke, and caused the now energized warehouse dust to further ignite, greatly multiplying the explosive force leveled on Die Glocke.

Thousands of tiny bits and pieces of warehouse debris rained down over them for what seemed like an eternity.

Ross slowly raised his head to see, and then stood up.

Through the smoke and chaos he narrowed his eyes surveying the destructive scene.

The warehouse was still standing, but now there was a huge gaping hole in the ancient metal roof.

Ross offered his hand to Lin and pulled her up.

"Come on," said Ross.

Together, Ross and Lin crept back into the Talstrasse warehouse.

The inside looked like it had been ravaged by a cyclone.

Ross moved towards the spot where the Nazi machine known as Die Glocke had stood.

The concrete immediately underneath where it had been was now a sheet of steaming, crystallized glass.

But there was nothing left of Die Glocke.

Ross slowly circled around, looking for any debris from the machine and any remains of Lugoff, anything at all.

He had witnessed countless explosions in his career, and viewed numerous blast scenes.

But in this case there simply was no trace left, of man or machine.

Lin spoke first.

"I don't see anything left of the machine or of him," she remarked. "Is that normal?"

Ross kept staring at the concrete floor where Die Glocke had stood.

He reached in his trousers pocket and pulled out two coins.

Ross didn't say a word as he knelt down on one knee and placed the coins on the crystallized surface.

"What's that?" asked Lin.

Ross uttered, "For the boatman."

EPILOGUE

In all history, there is no instance of a country having benefitted from prolonged warfare. Only one who knows the disastrous effects of a long war can realize the supreme importance of rapidly bringing it to a close.

Sun Tzu
544 — 496 BC
Chinese General

CHRISTMAS EVE TONIGHT

It's a cold night.

Large flakes of glistening white snow were gently falling and swirling around him.

The playful flakes encircled him, and merged with the rest of the frosty winter wonderland at his feet.

The soldier was uncomfortable, and stomped his feet on the frozen ground.

My God it's cold, he thought to himself.

Searching for the pocket on his newly purchased trench coat, he slid his hand in and automatically extracted a little red jewelry box.

He popped open the top and looked at the diamond ring. The shimmering overhead streetlamps made the diamond sparkle brilliantly against the darkness of the night.

He glanced down at the ring and thought about his life.

I have been colder.

Yes, he thought, *that time as a kid in Pennsylvania when I fell through the ice at Lake Somerset.*

That was extraordinarily cold!

He snapped the top back down on the jewelry box and replaced it, only this time in his suit coat pocket.

Ross's mind was whirling with thoughts.

He had done as Colonel Winbolt had ordered. He contacted the US Embassy and provided them an after action report that would keep them busy for the next year. The embassy brought in INTERPOL, with all their international police assets. INTERPOL brought in the Swiss Federal Office of Police, with all their cantonal cooperation. Now it was their jobs to sort through Lugoff's Swiss property holdings and finances. Since this case involved terrorism, money laundering, and crimes against humanity…everyone was happy.

No one was really surprised that the three bars of 1943 Nazi Reichsbank gold had completely vanished.

The damn Pakistani terrorists!

They must have had even more confederates at large doing their evil bidding!

But Ross kept quiet.

He had given Emanuel one Nazi gold bar to help pay for the reconstruction of his cousin's restaurant.

Emanuel was happy.

With a value of five hundred and sixty thousand US dollars, Emanuel's cousin, Lailani, could rebuild her Asiatisches Essen restaurant…and then some.

Ross gave the other Nazi gold bar to Lin. He helped her exchange it for cash and electronically transfer the funds into her credit union account.

A little G.I. Bill for when she goes back to college, he thought.

But where was the third bar of Nazi gold?

Ross had converted that particular bar into cash himself.

He then donated the entire sum, anonymously, to the Wounded Warrior Project.

That money would be used to help injured United States soldiers returning from the war.

It would be the antithesis of what Lugoff had been doing.

But he was still disconcerted.

He wondered if Die Glocke had actually been what Wolfram von Lugoff had said it was, a time machine.

He wondered if Lugoff had survived.

He wondered if Lugoff was traveling through the fourth dimension itself, invading the past or the present.

He wondered if Lugoff would go back and save his father and mother from their collective fates.

He wondered if Lugoff would somehow erase his past and create a better future for himself.

Ross was standing outside on the Bahnhofstrasse near Zurich's main railway station.

He had just completed his shopping at the exquisite Les Ambassadeurs Boutique, and was waiting for Lin.

Ross pressed his left thumb and forefinger to the bridge of his nose and squeezed, tightly closing his eyes. He shook his head and tried to clear his mind of all thoughts, except Lin.

Reaching into the back pocket of his trousers, Ross pulled out his wallet. He extracted the embossed business card of the psychiatrist he had been secretly seeing at Fort Meade.

Ross slowly ran his thumb over the edge of the card.

Then he ripped the card in two, and let the halves flutter like silent snowflakes to the wet pavement below.

If he needed therapy, he would get it from Lin.

Her passionate embrace would quench his fiery temper.

Her gentle eyes would soothe his wounded heart.

Her soft lips would calm his restless spirit.

Her unconditional love would rescue his tortured soul.

Lin Sparrow was all the therapy that James Ross would ever require.

It's Christmas Eve, he thought, *and tonight I'm going to ask the most important question of my life.*

Ross looked at his battered Benrus watch.

Its luminous blade hands told him it was twenty-one-hundred hours.

Nine o'clock, thought Ross.

Lin should be here by now.

No sooner had Ross's thoughts turned to Lin, than there she was, standing next to him in her new winter overcoat.

As if by magic.

"Hello James."

"Where did you come from?" asked a startled Ross, "I was just thinking about you. I didn't even see you walk up."

"I'm a witch, or didn't you know?" smiled Lin mischievously.

Ross laughed.

"You know, I've found a little restaurant around the corner that is supposed to have the best French onion soup in all of Switzerland. What do you say?"

"It sounds absolutely lovely," said Lin. "Let's go."

Ross offered his arm to Lin, and together they strolled down the Bahnhofstrasse towards the Brasserie Lipp restaurant.

The night was vibrantly alive with red and green twinkling Christmas lights everywhere. Silver strands of tinsel were strung across evergreen trees giving them a chandelier-type appearance. Merchant shop windows were warmly illuminated, displaying everything from windup toys to the latest designer fashions. An ocean of autos were beeping their horns and trying to avoid being the last one home for Christmas Eve.

It was the hustle and bustle of the merriest time of year in Switzerland.

Soon the young lovers were engulfed by a sea of other couples strolling together down the Bahnhofstrasse, enjoying the sights and sounds of the holiday season.

Small gusts of wind carrying wet flakes of snow swirled around them, and teased at them playfully.

Their breath was coming out in puffs as one, circling and disappearing skyward as they huddled closer, arm-in-arm with smiles on their faces.

It was a scene reminiscent of a Charles Dickens novel.

Ross's mind finally cleared of thoughts about Die Glocke and Wolfram von Lugoff.

He was now enjoying every second with Lin.

Soon Ross pointed with his finger, and they turned right onto Uraniastrasse. A few more meters and they arrived at their destination.

The Brasserie Lipp is a little French restaurant at number nine Uraniastrasse. It is one of Zurich's authentic French restaurants, and has taken on a type of cult status all its own. Its menu is famous for bourgeois bouillabaisse, fresh seafood, and of course authentic French onion soup.

"Willkommen," beamed the jovial maitre d'. "Welcome to the Brasserie Lipp!"

"Thank you sir," said Ross. "Ummm, I have a reservation for two, under the name of Ross."

"Yes of course mein Herr, of course."

Scanning his roster, the maitre d' found Ross's reservation.

"Ah yes, here it is mein Herr. Please follow me."

The maitre d' led Ross and Lin into the Elizabethan-styled elevator and escorted them up to the Jules Verne Panorama Bar on the top floor.

"Is this your first time at the Brasserie Lipp?" the maitre d' asked.

Ross answered, "Yes sir, it is."

"Well then, may I say you're in for a wonderful time here," chimed the maitre d'.

Opening the lift gate, the maitre d' said, "Here you are sir, just as you requested." Gesturing with his hands, he remarked, "You will love these incomparable views of Zurich. They are truly wunderbar."

The maitre d' led them to their table by a huge panoramic window.

"Please let me take your garments."

Lin elegantly slipped out of her overcoat and allowed the maitre d' to lift it off of her shoulders.

"Thank you," said Lin.

Ross pulled off his trench coat.

"Here you go. Thanks," said Ross.

Frantically, Ross ran his fingers through his thick shock of hair that always fell across his forehead. He tried to push the dark brown bangs away, but in a second they just fell back down again, only in more disarray.

The maitre d' quickly handed their garments over to a coat check girl, and then returned his attention to the couple.

"Mademoiselle," said the maitre d', as he pulled out and held an elegant chair for Lin to sit down.

Ross pulled out his own chair and sat down.

"Thank you sir," said Ross.

About ten dining tables were located in the Jules Verne Bar. They were strategically placed around the open center fireplace. The crackling fire added a nice warm glow to the already magnificent ambience of the room.

Ross was pleasantly amused at the cross-mixing of Swiss, German, and French culture and language.

"I will send your waiter right over," said the maitre d'.

The maitre d' clapped his hands and a waiter materialized at their table with two menus.

"Good evening, Mademoiselle et Monsieur" said the waiter, handing them each a menu.

The waiter was a young guy, perhaps only nineteen. He was tall and slender, with strikingly azure eyes. His hair was blonde and cut in a style reminiscent of the early 1960s Beatles mop tops. He had the long sleeves of his white silk shirt buttoned down to the wrists. They were covering up the magnificent tiger tattoos on both forearms of which he was obviously proud, but forbidden to reveal at work.

"Our specialties tonight are soufflé au fromage, crab au gratin, roast duck, and prime rib au jus."

"May I recommend, eh, perhaps an appetizer first, Monsieur?"

Ross had asked the next question at dozens of restaurants throughout the world. He enjoyed the routine and loved the responses. Mostly though, he loved the soup.

"Do you have French onion soup tonight?" inquired Ross.

The waiter looked up from his notepad and smiled.

"Bien sur, Monsieur! Why yes of course! The best French onion soup in all of Switzerland," he said proudly.

"Okay. We'll each have the French onion soup, with a large thin slice of cheese melted over the top," said Ross, returning the waiter's smile.

"And for the entrées, Monsieur?"

Ross looked at Lin and said, "We'll both have the prime rib au jus, avec haricots verts, potatoes au gratin, et salade vert avec balsamic vinaigrette, s'il vous plait."

The waiter rapidly wrote it all down onto his notepad.

"And may I say Monsieur, your French is quite excellent," said the waiter, giving Ross the okay symbol.

"Merci," said Ross smiling.

"And what will you have to drink, Monsieur?"

"Bring us a bottle of Moet et Chandon please," said Ross.

"Ah yes, very good Monsieur."

The waiter finished writing, bowed, and rapidly shuffled away.

Ross reached into the pocket of his dark gray pinstriped suit coat and pulled out the small red jewelry box.

He slid it across the table to Lin.

Lin saw the box and clasped her hands together over her heart in a slightly exaggerated surprise expression.

She smiled and opened the tiny box.

Inside was a one carat diamond, set in a four prong eighteen karat gold ring.

Lin smiled and blushed.

"Oh, it's beautiful James. It's simply beautiful."

A curious gentle glow overcame Lin, and she asked, "James is this what I *think* it is?"

Ross thought for a second.

He reached out and held Lin's hands in his.

He took the ring and slid it onto the third finger of her left hand.

"Lin, I love you. I want to be together with you forever."

Lin looked into James Ross's piercing dark brown eyes. She looked at the shards of hair hanging across his forehead that would never stay in place. She looked at the lips that had always spoken the truth to her.

“Together?” asked Lin.

“Together,” said Ross.

“Together, forever?” asked Lin breathlessly.

“Yes. Together, forever,” said Ross.

Then Ross asked the question that he had never asked a woman before. It was the question he thought he might never ask in this lifetime. It was the question that has been asked by young men for thousands of years.

“Lin, I love you. Will you marry me?”

Lin gasped and without realizing it, held her breath in for a few seconds. A single tear trickled down her cheek.

She finally let her breath out and started to speak.

“James …”

Just then the waiter returned with the French onion soup.

THE END

ABOUT THE AUTHOR

Bernard Cenney retired from the United States Army as a Lieutenant Colonel after more than twenty-eight years in uniform. He considers it a privilege to have served his country throughout numerous command and staff assignments the world over. He makes Texas his home.

www.ingramcontent.com/pod-product-compliance
Lightning Source LLC
Chambersburg PA
CBHW030422310726
48979CB00009B/1578/J

* 9 7 8 1 7 3 6 2 4 5 1 7 0 *